EVERNIGHT PUBLISHING ®

www.evernightpublishing.com

Copyright© 2021

Sam Crescent

Editor: Audrey Bobak

Cover Art: Jay Aheer

ISBN: 978-0-3695-0314-5

MONSTERS' GIFT

MONSTERS' GIFT

Crude Hill High, 2

Sam Crescent

Copyright © 2021

⟨∙◆∙⟩

Prologue

Caleb

I'd never felt like this.

The pain was unreal.

As I climbed into the car where my friends were, none of us spoke. What was the point in speaking? We'd just put our woman on a private jet with a whole new life mapped out. One that only our fathers knew about.

Gael stared out the window. River had the tip of the blade he'd stolen from Emily pressing into his thigh. From this angle, I knew he was pushing it in, slowly sinking it into his flesh. The tension of his jaw was a clear indicator.

Vadik's hands were clenched into fists.

None of us were used to this level of pain. River probably was, but I couldn't seem to stop it. All I wanted to do was scream and shout.

I sat behind the wheel without knowing what to say. There was nothing. No words.

Our entire life had just been put on a jet and was now making a new one without us. We didn't know her brand-new name or where she'd be. She could be in some town close by, or another country.

"Do you think they'll keep their word?" Gael asked.

"Yes," River said. "They wouldn't lie to us."

"Oh, really? They were more than willing to kill the only woman we've ever loved." Gael slammed the palm of his hand against the car window. "Fuck this. Fuck them. Why did we have to give her up?"

"We couldn't allow them to kill her." I didn't know why I was making excuses. Gael knew why we'd done it.

"There's four of us. We could have taken them. This is all fucking horseshit. I don't … she was … I don't…" Gael stopped speaking. One glance in the rearview mirror showed that he struggled with tears.

We'd gone through so much together, but I couldn't recall any of us crying. It was kind of sad when I thought about it.

No tears.

We'd all accepted how our lives had turned out. It sucked.

"Do you just accept this?" Gael asked.

"I accept that we made the right choice with her. We made the choice she needed."

"It wasn't the right choice," he said. "Not the right choice at all." He climbed out of the car just as the jet took off. We all followed him, standing by his side as Emily was taken from us.

"She's going to think we abandoned her," Vadik said.

"We know we didn't," I said. "We have given her the best chance. The best opportunity to live. Try to think about what she's now got. She's got a full life ahead of her. One she's going to enjoy more than anything." I didn't know if I was explaining this well or just trying to give a more involved reasoning for why we'd let our woman go. "She would know we loved her."

I didn't know how long we stood in that same spot. Cars honked at us as we stood in the way at the airport, but we ignored them. Gael stared up at the sky as if he imagined Emily magically sprouting wings and flying.

I didn't know what to say or do. I felt completely helpless, and this was all my fault.

Finally, I didn't know what happened, but Gael stepped back.

From the look on his face, the boy he'd once been had just faded. I saw the anger, the rage, the deep-seated pain. He didn't say anything as he climbed inside.

One by one, we got back into the car, but I knew we were not the same men.

We were finally the monsters our fathers had always hoped we'd be.

Chapter One

Emily

I sang the birthday song in my head, staring at the cupcake with one candle aglow. Seven years had passed since I'd been Emily Crane. Every single part of my past life had been extinguished.

Now I was Amelia Coast. Ashley was now my sister, Harper.

I still found it hard to think of myself as Amelia. We still lived in the apartment I'd first woken up in. According to my records, I'd graduated high school, and to pass the time, I'd taken a couple of college courses at night.

Ashley attended culinary classes and worked at a restaurant about five minutes from where we lived, while I worked at a local supermarket. The job wasn't very exciting, but after work, I'd then go to my night job of cleaning. I liked having two jobs. Ashley believed I worked too much, but it was much better than sitting around the house moping. I did that a lot regardless. Like now.

Twenty-five years old and my heart still ached for the men I couldn't have. I hated myself and my weakness. I should be able to forget about them, but I couldn't. Caleb, River, Vadik, and Gael. Four boys, no, they'd been four men, even back in high school. I rubbed at my chest, the pain still very much there.

In and out.

I tried to take deep breaths, but it failed. It always failed. Tears filled my eyes and because I was alone, I allowed them to fall.

Ashley didn't need me to be strong right now. Whenever I was around her, I always found myself fighting to be strong for her. She didn't need me to be anything but myself, which I found a huge relief. I didn't want to be anyone else.

Just myself, trying to focus on the now.

With the tears sliding down my cheeks, I stared at the candle, wondering what they were doing. Had they moved on? Like their fathers, did they have a new woman? Did they have sons of their own?

At the sound of the door opening, I quickly swiped at the tears on my cheeks.

"Hey, it's me. I'm home. You do not even know the day I've had it has been so freaking hectic but so much fun. I have learned so much." The light turned on as Ashley came into the room, carrying a whole load of bags on her arms and a white box in her hand. "Oh, no, you didn't think I'd forgotten, did you?"

I got to my feet as Ashley made her way toward me. "No, no, no, not that tiny cupcake. It's your birthday. This isn't the time for you to be just one single cupcake. We are not watching our figures here."

Ashley had once been the thinner of the two of us. Now she had the curves and I struggled to eat. I'd tried. Eating had no appeal to me, but Ashley did everything she could to help me. She was a damn good cook, and I did feel bad.

One day, she'd come home all excited about how she was going to cook on camera and upload it onto a social media site, to which I reminded her that we couldn't exist online. She'd instantly deflated and I'd felt like the worst kind of person. She instead learned to cook and I'd film her on my cell phone, and we'd watch it.

If it hadn't been for my father, I just knew she'd be awesome. She was made to be in front of the camera. Her smile, her charm, her wit, it all came across as she cooked. I knew when she wished for something, it was to be a cook. She was so passionate about food.

I watched as she blew out the candle, pushed her long brown hair off her face, and slid the white box in front of me. Opening the lid, I saw it was a chocolate cake. Possibly fudgy.

"And I got ice cream." She rushed away and came back seconds later with a tub of vanilla ice cream. The good kind with vanilla specks in it.

I smiled.

"Oh, not finished."

She produced some birthday candles, one in the shape of a two and the other a five. Then I watched as she struck the match and lit each one before going to turn off the lights. "Now, don't forget to make a wish."

For several seconds, I stared at the candles, wondering what I could wish for. What would be worth the words that could possibly come true? Nothing seemed to be of any value to me.

What was the point?

I didn't have my men. There was no one to love.

Wrapping my arms around myself, I looked at the burning candle and knew that come this time next year, I didn't want to feel this way. I hated the pain, the sadness. Ashley didn't deserve it, and for the last seven years, that was all I'd been, sad.

My life kept on whizzing by and I didn't have a single good memory. Well, I did, but I was wasting mine, and I couldn't allow that to happen anymore.

Rather than wish for something I couldn't have, I made one plan: to be happy. That was what I was going to do. No more wallowing. No more wishing for something that would never happen. It wasn't lost on me that I'd spent seven years craving to be back in the arms of the men at Crude Hill high, and yet while I was there, I wanted to be anywhere but.

No more.

I was going to move on.

Blowing out the candles, I felt slightly different.

Ashley clapped her hands, cheered for me, and giggled. "Do you feel any different?" she asked, going to turn the light on.

"Yeah, I do." I smiled at her.

She came back. "Now I think it's only fair that we have cake, then I'm cooking you a delicious meal."

"You don't have to do that. We could go out dancing if you'd like?"

Ashley put a hand to her chest. "Really? You'd come out dancing with me?"

"Hell, yeah, why not? I'd like to." She'd tried to get me to go out dancing so many times. "I've been a sucky roommate."

"Don't," Ashley said. She offered me the knife to cut the cake. "You've been what you've needed to be. I've never felt … you know. I don't know what it's like to want to be with someone that being apart is like a pain in itself."

Now I felt even worse. She hadn't experienced love, and it was all my fault.

"I'm so sorry," I said.

"Stop." She chuckled. "I've gone out dancing. I've been on dates, and believe me, I haven't met anyone who has made me want to drop my panties."

"Just so you know, I didn't want to drop my panties for them for a long time. I actually wanted to kill them."

"We shouldn't talk about them. Not on your birthday."

I slid a slice of cake toward her and she dolloped out the softened ice cream. She ran to get spoons, handing me one. I made sure I had a nice piece of cake and some ice cream before having a taste. I closed my eyes. The vanilla and dark fudgy chocolate were perfect.

"You made this, didn't you?"

"Yes, I stayed late last night at the restaurant. What do you think?"

"You're really good."

"I've been trying to perfect this recipe for so long." She took a bite herself and closed her eyes. "This is so good."

"Are you not happy with it?"

"Oh, I am, but I'm already moving on to my next challenge."

Ashley had an entire stack of notebooks full of her ideas. There were plenty of disasters in there, but she was never put off. Her enthusiasm was addictive. I finished my slice off within a few bites, and when she offered me some more, I accepted.

"I'll cook us something when we get back from dancing."

We ate another slice and then it was time to get ready.

After heading into my bedroom, I went to my wardrobe and looked through my clothes. I had a couple of black dresses, and I picked the one that came to my knees. When I'd bought them, I'd been a bit bigger, but fortunately, I still had the tits to pull it off.

Ashley was already waiting for me when I joined her in our living room.

"Damn, you look hot. How about we skip men and make out?" Ashley asked.

I rolled my eyes. "You don't have to keep being so nice."

"I do. It's your birthday. What better way to be nice?"

"I'm not looking for a date, or any guy for that

matter."

"Stop being a party pooper. It's not fair." Ashley stuck her tongue out. "Now, let's go and party like our lives depend on it."

Our lives didn't depend on anything. Grabbing my bag, I followed Ashley out of our apartment, letting her lock up. We linked arms as we made our way out into the night. People were already milling about in the street. We walked a couple of feet away from our apartment, and Ashley hailed us a taxi. It took a few minutes but finally, someone was willing to stop.

I smiled, relieved as I didn't want to have to walk all the way to the nightclub. I didn't know where she wanted to take us, but right now, all I wanted to do was forget about everything and everyone. Especially four guys back at a town I once loathed.

Once inside the car, Ashley kept the driver entertained, allowing me to sit back, relax, and just focus on the passing world. I didn't know if this would be the biggest mistake in the world.

Going out for my birthday had sounded like fun, but now, I didn't think it would be.

After half an hour, Ashley grabbed my hand, leading me out into the night. She waved at the bouncer at the front door, and much to my surprise, we were allowed in.

"I know Philip. He's a good guy. He comes into the restaurant all the time and I helped him with proposing to his fiancée." Ashley tugged me deep into the nightclub. The lights were all down. The music was just a jumble of notes filling the air.

People danced on the main floor. No one seemed to have any rhythm, but no one cared.

Before I had a chance to turn her down, Ashley pulled me onto the dance floor and made me work my hips. It wasn't so bad. Kind of fun actually. No one expected anything from me, which was a welcome relief.

Pushing all my previous thoughts out of my head, I let myself go, dancing and enjoying myself. It wasn't too hard to do. Not when I finally let everything go and just enjoyed the feelings. It was nice. Freeing.

We stopped to get some drinks, then started back dancing. A couple of guys tried to hit on us, but Ashley sent them on their way. Tonight was about me, apparently.

Finally, we were both exhausted and found a booth that made it a little more private. The music was still too loud, but we could at least talk to one another.

"This is so much fun, am I right?" Ashley asked.

"Yeah. It's great. You know, I wouldn't mind if you wanted to go out on a date."

Ashley waved her hand in front of me. "Please, I don't want to even think about guys right now. I'm focused on my career. Guys are like totally boring." She blew out a breath as she looked out across the dance floor.

I reach across and take hold of her hand. "This is our life now, Ash. We're not going back there. Ever. This is all we've got."

"I get that, and guess what, the only person I want to spend my life with is you. I don't care about men or relationships." She shrugged. "I really need to pee. How about we have another drink and then go and get some food?"

"Yeah, I'm game. I'll wait here."

"Thanks."

Ashley slid out of the booth and I sat, waiting for her. She disappeared from sight, and I ran my fingers across the table. It had been nice to dance, but my feet were killing me. Regardless of what anyone said, there was no good way to dance in heels. They were horrible death contraptions.

I couldn't wait to take them off and give myself a foot massage.

Someone sat in the booth and I'd been so busy looking out across the crowd, I didn't pay attention.

I was about to tell them I'd be going, but all the words died in my throat as I saw who sat opposite me. I hadn't seen him in seven years. The night that had changed it all.

Earl Valentine. The man my father had intended to sell me to. My virginity. Not me. I wasn't the commodity, my precious hymen had been. Of course, realizing what my father planned, I'd slept with not one but two of my men, and I didn't regret it.

Staring at him now, I knew we were in danger. I glanced in the direction of where Ashley had gone.

"She's safe," he said.

I clenched my hands into tight fists. Seven years of being all alone had made me sloppy. I didn't have anything to back me up. No protection of any kind.

I didn't know what the fuck to do.

"What are you doing here?"

"It's a free country, and London is such a wonderful city. Have you seen it at Christmas?"

He knew damn well I'd seen it at that time of year. Fucker.

I didn't like this.

Even though I'd been miserable, I enjoyed not living in fear. I no longer constantly put my back to any room. I took my time where I went. Right now, I was pissed off. I hated this feeling.

In a few short seconds, he'd made me ache for the freedom I'd possessed.

"What do you want?"

"Now that's a rather interesting question, isn't it? Originally, I was promised a virgin woman. Then, of course, that was taken from me, and in its place as a peace offering, I was granted an alignment with the Monsters that saw me double my empire."

"If that's the case, why are you here? How do you know about me?" I wasn't going to bring Ashley into this. I wanted to try to make him forget she even existed. I didn't know how I was going to do that.

She was an innocent. My father had brought her and her mother into the limelight. If it hadn't been for Caleb, River, Gael, and Vadik, I knew she'd be dead as well.

Her mother hadn't made it.

That was the curse of betraying the Monsters. There was no way out once you sank into that pool of despair, and my dad had done that, dragging us all down. There was no mercy.

In my old world, mercy was a weakness.

There was no way the Monsters would be seen as weak.

I waited, watching him. "Have you been sent here to finally kill me?"

"How scared you sound, Emily."

I didn't correct him. Emily was no longer my name.

"You're still incredibly beautiful. You've lost a lot of weight." His gaze moved toward where Ashley had walked. "But your friend, she has really blossomed into one hell of a lady, and I know for a fact she's a virgin."

"You leave her out of this."

"You'd like that, would you? To leave her out of this. I'm still owed a virgin."

"You got your empire. No one owes you anything."

"Ah, but you see, just as quickly an empire can be created, it can also be taken. It's been seven long years since you were last in Crude Hill. I can tell you now, girl, what was once there is not what's there now."

"It's none of my concern."

"But it is. People thought they had seen the real evil of this world. What they didn't know was by taking you away, they would unleash hell as we know it. The Monsters' Crew were tame before. Your boys, they are … let's just say, I'm hiding out."

I frowned. "I have no idea what you're talking about."

"Crude Hill has entered its darkest days yet. Pain and suffering come to many, and it's your boys who have taken their fathers' empire to the next level."

"Are they dead?" I asked. Not that it mattered.

Earl shook his head. "They're not dead, but I have a feeling they will regret what they unleashed. Their sons overthrew them, and now they are nothing more than shells. Only you can bring them back from this darkness."

"That's not my life anymore."

"Life or not, if you love them, do you want them to face death without telling them once that you loved them?"

I opened my mouth but he stood up. "Tell your friend I said hello."

"You leave her alone."

He was suddenly in my face. "Don't forget who you are, Emily. Just because you escaped my grasp doesn't mean your friend will succeed. I want a virgin, and she looks way too tasty to ignore."

In the next second, he was gone. Seconds later, Ashley returned from the bathroom, and I grabbed her hand, making my way out into the night. We had to get out of the nightclub. It was wrong of us to even go there. I knew that now. We'd fucked up, but I wouldn't make that mistake again.

I had to get her to safety. It was my only priority.

Ashley didn't stop me or question me as to why I was in such a hurry to get back to the safety of our home.

Earl was watching us, I just knew it, but what was more, I couldn't prove it, which I hated. The first night I'd let my guard down and look what happened. I wasn't going to make that mistake again.

Chapter Two

Emily

"Do you want to tell me what the hell is going on?" Ashley asked.

I slammed our apartment door closed and flicked the lock into place. Normally, that was all I did, but today, I wasn't in the mood, so one by one, I bolted the place up. We had the main lock, along with three bolts above, and four down, leading to the ground. Looking through the peephole, I checked to see if anyone watched us, but I couldn't see anything.

"Now you're scaring me, and that's not funny. This isn't fair."

My heart raced. I heard the fear in Ashley's voice and I knew it wasn't nice of me to just act this way.

Taking a deep breath, I turned toward her. She had her arms folded across her breasts, her gaze focused on me, and I knew she was pissed. "Are you going to tell me what's going on?"

"I … yes, I want to."

"Then what is the problem?" she asked.

Running fingers through my hair, I looked around at what we had. I fucking hated this. "While you went to the bathroom, something happened."

"No shit. I already figured that out. You know, with us practically running back home. We didn't call a taxi." She leaned down, taking off her heels one by one. "It doesn't take a genius to work out that you've got some serious issues, and now I'm pissed. My feet are killing me."

"Earl Valentine."

At the mention of his name, she went pale. "What?"

"That's what happened. He ... stopped by the booth."

Gone were the anger and blame, replaced by concern. This was one of the reasons why I loved Ashley. She never, ever held a grudge. She was so damn sweet and I loved her so much. She was the sister I never had.

We'd been through hell together, and it looked like we were about to go through a hell of a lot more.

"He's the guy your father sold you to, right?"

I nodded.

"What does he want?" she asked.

"I honestly don't know. He told me that ... they'd been more monsters than anything else. They've taken over from their dads and that they regret giving them the choice about me. I'm sorry. I ... I didn't want to ruin our night out. I was loving it."

Ashley rushed toward me, cupping my face. "Don't you worry about it. I mean it. I can't believe you were on your own with that asshole and I wasn't there." She growled. "I'm pissed at myself now."

I put a hand to my chest.

Within seconds, I was in her arms and she was stroking my hair. Panic rose. I hadn't had a panic attack in so long. Ashley had learned long ago how to get me out of them, or at least to stop them from being worse than they needed to be. She'd been my lifeline.

"I'm here. I've got you. You're safe. Nothing bad is going to happen."

Even though I didn't believe her, just being in the comfort of her arms, and listening to her, helped to stop the attack from building.

"We're good?" Ashley asked.

"I'm good. Thank you."

"Don't thank me. Wow, I thought you were going

to lose yourself." Ashely kissed my head. "I'm going to make you dinner. It's still your birthday and that asshole isn't ruining it for you."

"He knows where we are." I felt like I needed to remind her of what the hell was going on.

"I get that, but he's part of the past. It doesn't matter what he says or does. He's not going to ruin our lives. We've got each other, Em. That's all that matters."

"We're Amelia and Harper, remember?"

"I know you're panicking, but stop it. It's not right. None of this is going to help us. You know this. We all know this."

I ran a hand down my face. "Fine. Fine."

"Good. You know I'm right."

I didn't know at all. I had no idea what made her right or not. The truth was all I knew was how scary this was. After all this time, I didn't for a second think I would have to deal with my past.

If it had been Caleb, River, Gael, or Vadik, that would have been different. They were a past I'd wanted. I'd lost them before I'd even realized they were gone.

Kicking off my shoes, I followed Ashley into the kitchen and sat at the island in the center as she rummaged around, looking for ingredients to use. One of her favorite things to eat was pasta and she went out of her way to make a different sauce each time.

Today, it looked like we were going with a garlic and pepper sauce. It was watching Ashley like this that I wished we didn't have the risk of someone trying to find and kill us. Ashley would have made one hell of a cook. As it was, she'd given up all her dreams for this. She had a wonderful personality as well. People would adore her.

If there was ever one thing I could give my friend, it would be something like this.

Ashley hummed as she filled a saucepan with

water and placed it on the stove. I just watched. This was what I did. I'd never make it as a cook, while Ashley, she was superb. I'd gotten really lucky with her as a friend.

"Thank you," I said.

She turned toward me. "What for?"

"For being the best friend anyone could ever ask for. For being you. You could have left me a long time ago."

She giggled. "Don't be silly. This is your birthday and I won't have you talking like that. It's not fun. This is supposed to be fun." She turned her back to me. "I don't care who this man is, he's not going to spoil this for us. It has taken us too damn long to find any semblance of happiness, okay? Don't let them win."

I took a deep breath. "I wish I was so confident."

"Look, I get that this is bad news for both of us. It's not what we wanted, but there is nothing we can do about it. He's rich, right?"

I nodded.

"Then let's hope he gets bored with the risk of what kind of hell he can bring to us, and move on. What do you say?" Ashley offered me a smile. "And the next time he turns up, keep him around and I'll gut him myself." She held a knife up. "And you know how deadly I can be with a knife."

I laughed. There wasn't much else I could do. "Cook for me, woman," I said.

Ashley winked at me but went back to slicing the garlic. Her hand moved so rapidly but not once did she take off her fingers. I couldn't tear my gaze away. She was so expert.

Once she'd finished with all the garlic, she grabbed another pan. This was magic in the kitchen.

She poured enough olive oil in the pan to coat the bottom, probably more than I ever would use normally.

This was what made her food so good. She wasn't afraid of the ingredients.

Before putting the oil on the heat, she added in all the garlic, then put the heat on low. The water for the pasta had come to a boil.

Again, so much salt, it made me wonder if she was trying to turn me into a fish. After that, she moved back to her pot with the garlic. Lots of black pepper was added, and she quickly rushed to the cupboard to grab another spice.

I didn't see what this one was.

There was a time I'd catch her talking to herself, or pretending there was a camera watching her. This was how I knew her dream. When she didn't think I was around, she'd still do it, and it made me sad to think of everything she'd lost.

Before I knew what was happening, she'd drained the pasta, poured it into the other pot. More work was happening but her back was to me.

Within a matter of minutes, with plates piled high, we moved to our sofa, sat down with the food and forks, and ate.

"I had hoped tonight would be wonderful for you," she said.

"It was. There was nothing you could do."

She sighed. "Doesn't help, though, does it? It drives me crazy that after all this time, all it takes is one appearance from a guy, and we're panicking."

I took a bite of my pasta and closed my eyes. "This is really good."

"This is your way of avoiding the subject."

"This is my way of dealing."

Ashely moved so she faced me. "Okay, you now have my full attention. I'm right here. Tell me what you want to tell me. I know there's something on your mind."

I kept facing forward. There was nothing to discuss, not really.

"Em, I know you. We've done this so often. Don't try to fool me."

"It's nothing."

"I mean it."

"Okay, fine." I turned to look at her. "I'm curious, okay. We all know they were a pain in the ass when we were in high school, but now, aren't you a little curious?" I asked.

"As to how bad they got?"

"Yes."

"I don't know. I do try to not think about everything that happened back then. I always felt it was easier."

I groaned. "You're right. So totally right."

"It doesn't make me right, Em. You know that. They were yours. All four of them." She frowned. "It still seems weird to think of four guys belonging to you. I know this wasn't easy for them, but they gave you up because they loved you."

"Yeah, right." I snorted. "They got what they wanted and passed me up."

"You told me everything that happened. There's four of them and you slept with two. Working on your theory, they all had to have been with you, to pass you up."

I sighed. "That's not helping."

"They did this to protect you. I don't think that's anything to be afraid of."

"What if they're here?"

"In London?"

"Yeah."

"Not possible." Ashley slurped up some of her pasta.

"Why?"

"If they had been here, you'd have known about it. They wouldn't have been able to stay away from you. If they ever come to London, you'll be the first person to know about it." She winked at me. "I remember the way they all looked at you. It was like you were the sunshine and they gravitated toward you. One day, I hope someone looks at me like that, but I doubt I will ever allow myself to fall in love with someone."

This made me pause as I watched her. "Why?"

"Why what?"

"Why won't you give love a chance?"

"Come on, Em. Think about it. I can never allow myself to fall in love with a guy."

"And again, I'm wondering why the hell not." I wasn't being stupid.

"You're being stubborn."

"Hello, I'm not the one who's thinking of never being with a guy."

Ashely put her food down. It was only half eaten. She held her hand up. "First, you don't even look at men. You turn down dates when you have no reason to. Second, if you love someone with all of your heart and soul, then you've got to be honest with them. The person I fall in love with, I already have to lie to them, Em. I'm not me. The me that I am is with you. Everything else, it's all a lie."

"You're not lying."

"I guess you don't understand."

"I do," I said. "I just want what is best for you, that's all."

My friend reached out, taking my hand. "And I love you for it. I do. But I'm a realist. I know there are going to be sacrifices to keep us safe. This is the risk we took. I'm glad I did because I love you. You're the best friend and sister I always dreamed about. I'm not going to let anyone or anything come between us. We've got this."

I put my food down and threw myself at my best friend, holding her close. "You're the best present anyone could ever want. I love you so much."

We held each other for several minutes.

"Now, I'm starving. You don't think after all of that touchy-feely crap I wouldn't eat. I need food and I need it now."

I laughed along with her, just thankful she was in my life. If the four monsters from my past got anything right, it was bringing her with me to take care of me, and for that, I couldn't hate them.

****

Caleb

Back in Crude Hill

The sound of screams filled the air. There was a time the sounds bothered me, whereas now, I loved it. They made me feel, and that, nowadays was more important than anything else.

"Please, I beg you, please."

Getting up from my seat, I held the whiskey in my hand as I watched Gael and River each take a turn slicing into the man. He was a cop, one who had been working both sides. He thought to tame us monsters. He'd once worked for our parents, being the perfect little mole within the force. We'd long taken over and people needed to realize our parents were like Santa Claus. We were anything but. We were the real deal. People feared us more than they ever did our fathers. It was kind of funny when I thought about it.

The man bled, and Vadik chuckled, drawing my attention. He had a girl sitting in his lap. More important, it was the cop's daughter. She was twenty years old, but she knew where real loyalty was. When she heard what her father had tried to do, frame us and bring the real law to our town, she'd come directly to us. Like all good minions, she was rewarded. This girl would have the mark of the Monsters. She'd be untouchable. It was rare for us to give our symbol to a girl, to anyone.

It was so hard to find loyalty in this day and age.

River stepped back, unzipped his fly, and began to piss all over the cop, who tried to swing out of the way.

His blood painted our floor so beautifully.

Gael did the same, and I heard a feminine squeal. Turning toward Vadik, I saw him kiss our guest, his hand cupping her tit. I waited, wondering what he would do. When he was done kissing her, and the girl in question had her legs spread, Vadik removed her from his lap and sent her on her merry way.

There would be no fucking tonight. There hadn't been any fucking in a long time.

We'd all tried, though.

Emily's memory was just too damn strong. She was in our blood.

Her presence was gone, long gone, but we all still craved her more than anything else.

Gael, seeing that Vadik still struggled, attacked our man again, this time, stabbing him repeatedly. With his anger, he rarely was easy to rein in, not that I wanted to. Our fathers had given us all an ultimatum, and well, that had been their mistake.

I smiled when I thought of my father, all of our fathers. They had believed we were controllable. Their biggest mistake was taking the one person who could keep us in line. Rather than bring her back, they'd stood their ground. They were old fools. Now at the ripe age of twenty-five, we'd taken their empire from them.

They were all still alive. We couldn't exactly kill them, at least not yet. The fun was in showing each one how much they had fucked up. The mistakes they'd made. This town once had been a town for enemies to walk freely with the risk. Now, it was no more than a bloodbath.

We didn't allow them to hide their true colors. We didn't play pretend.

Nightmares were not confined to the dead of night.

It was real. Every single day.

"He's dead," I said, bored. This was the problem with letting Gael play. He always took it way too far, and look what happened. Our fun was gone for the day.

"Fuck," Gael said. "Damn, he didn't last now, did he?" He stood up, wiping the blood on his jeans.

Gone were the suits that had once been the symbol of good business. We only played the part for all our legal shit, but we paid good men to keep an eye on that. There was a time we'd have enjoyed running the businesses, playing both sides. Ever since Emily was taken from us, we'd only been content in the darkness. There was no room for light in our lives.

"He would have lasted if you showed any kind of control," I said, draining the last of my whiskey. This was damn good stuff, but I wanted more.

"Oh, really, and you think you've got better control?" he asked.

"I know I do because I get to entertain myself for a lot longer than you." I raised my brow as he came toward me.

We could fight. We were our only real competition. No one had been able to best us, and we'd killed one too many soldiers. When we beat the shit out of each other, our only agreement was no killing blows. It was a rush to hold back on one another.

There were times, though, I knew Gael and I wanted to kill Vadik and River. They had gotten a taste of her. They'd felt her tight cunt and knew how perfect she was. What did we get? Nothing. A few stolen kisses and the chance to watch. Nothing of any real importance. It pissed me off. Even as we'd taken over from our fathers, we all knew they still held the power and control over Emily's life. Even if we were to kill everyone we knew associated with them, more would randomly appear. We were fucked no matter which way we worked it.

Emily's life hung in the balance and none of us were willing to take that risk. Least of all, me.

"I guess you were always too quick. Never savoring anything," I said, trying to goad Gael.

"Not tonight," River said, pulling his blade from the man on the floor.

"Don't even think to tell me what to do." I swallowed my drink and stared at River, daring him to push me.

Of course, he would. Why not? He knew how angry I was. They all did. Most of my life I'd been lied to. We'd finally found a woman to complete us and what happened? Yeah, she was taken away from us.

I'd tried to find ways around it, but so far, all I'd come up with was nothing. No way of making this right.

I wanted Emily. I craved her. She was in my blood. My need was focused only on her.

"You want to do this again?"

Some of the new scars on my body were the result of fighting River. I'd made him use those blades in our fight. Feeling them hurt my skin gave me such a rush. He looked at me now, bored.

After I threw my empty glass toward him, he stepped out of the way.

Silence filled the air.

Tension mounted.

"Not tonight," River said.

"I don't give a flying fuck what you want."

"You think I don't know what tonight is?" River asked, shouting back. He'd started to turn his back on me after I'd thrown the glass, but now I had his attention again. "We all know what tonight is."

"Fuck you."

"It's her birthday."

I shook my head, not wanting to talk about it.

"You want to fight and blame me, go ahead. It doesn't change the fact we all fucked up."

"Would she even want us now?" Vadik asked, making us all pause.

I turned toward him. He held a glass between his fingers, staring into his drink. He looked a little lost. His obsession was still in place. I'd seen the haven he'd created. The shrine he devoted to Emily. The pictures he constantly drew to make her memory feel more alive. I'd even seen a couple of drawings of her naked. It made me wonder if they were true to memory.

"What the fuck did you say?" Gael asked.

Vadik laughed, downing his drink. Like the other glass, he threw it onto the floor. We had cleaners to come and take care of our messes. I hadn't cleaned up a single thing in years. It was beneath me.

"You think she'd want to be here after everything we've done?" Vadik looked at all of us. "When we had her, we were small fishes in a shark tank."

"Now we're the sharks," River said.

"No, we're the pieces of shit that pull the sharks out of the ocean and torture them," Vadik said. "Look at us. We use women. We kill people for fun. Yet, no matter what we do, we cannot find a way to bring her back. That's what we're looking for. We're trying to find our woman for us all." He sighed. "Me, I wouldn't take me back."

"Fuck this shit!" I turned on my heel, about to walk out of the room, but came to a stop when I saw a man in an expensive suit, looking mightily smug. I recognized him and instantly, I wanted to kill him.

I charged toward him, landing a blow, to which he laughed. We went down and as I straddled him, he grabbed my arms and shoved me back. As I got to my feet, Gael, Vadik, and River surrounded me. All four of us united together against our enemy. I was ready to fuck him up.

"Earl Valentine," Vadik said, spitting the word out.

"What the fuck are you doing here?" Gael asked.

River already had a knife out and was ready to strike. "Just say one more word and I'll gut you."

Earl looked at each one of us and laughed.

He was the first person to ever dare laugh at us. I looked at my guys and waited. We'd all be perfectly happy killing this fucker. He'd struck a deal with our fathers, and when we took over, that agreement had been severed.

My hand clenched into a fist. I craved to feel his bones break at my touch. It would be totally satisfying.

He sighed and glanced at the mess we'd made on the floor.

"They weren't wrong about you. So very uncivilized." He tutted. "You know, I figured you would take offense to my arrangement with your fathers. Don't get me wrong, I wanted a virgin pussy, but they tripled my fortune with taking my shipments of product."

To the outside world, Earl Valentine appeared to be an upstanding citizen. He had multiple empires in shipping and media. However, what people didn't know was he was also in the trafficking business. He made dirty deals on the sale of human flesh.

Just thinking of what this fucker could have done to our girl made my skin crawl. He wanted a virgin, but that deal had come off the table. Instead, our fathers had used his fleet and reputation to help transport guns and drugs, not to mention embezzling money, cleaning it.

They had all become rich, and with every day that passed, and each dollar earned, we had grown even more hostile.

"We've already told you the deal is completely off the table," I said.

Gael took a step toward the man.

He had the audacity to move toward our whiskey. Our really expensive brand. He poured himself a glass in one of the few remaining glasses we hadn't smashed. I'd lost count of the number of glasses and bottles we had to replace.

Gael wasn't a whiskey man. He preferred vodka.

Me, I just wanted to numb every single part of me. It helped me to sleep. A cranky me was not a good image.

Staring at this man, I saw blood. I wanted to sever every single limb I could get my hands on. He was everything I hated and even more. There would be no loss at his death.

"I have an agreement I think you would all be more than willing to be part of," Earl said.

I folded my arms and burst out laughing. "You think there is something I'd want from you?"

He reached into his pocket, and we all tensed. However, Earl only had his cell phone. It showed a video, which he pressed play to, and we saw Ashley and Emily.

I couldn't tear my gaze away. They were in a nightclub and it looked like they didn't have a clue they were being filmed. I didn't care about Ashley. The only person to hold my interest was the blonde. So beautiful. She'd lost way too much weight and even though she wore a little makeup, I saw the tiredness on her face.

Emily.

She needed us.

The video came to a stop.

"She is such a beautiful woman now. Ripe for the taking."

"You piece of fucking shit," River said, about to charge forward. As one, Gael, Vadik, and I stopped him.

Earl stared at us, the silence mounting with every passing second. "I don't appreciate being attacked."

"Tell us what you want and then get the fuck out," Gael said.

"Simple. I can make it so you can have Emily. I know what your fathers did. The men they've got tailing her, waiting for the sign to kill. I know everything."

"If you knew everything, why didn't you come to us before now?" I asked.

"Simple, there wasn't anything I wanted. Now, there is."

"You're not getting Emily."

"Oh, please, she's spoiled goods. When I made a deal with Crane, I didn't leave any error for him. I wanted a virgin. An untouched woman. Emily has you four and I have no wish to follow you."

I stared at him, waiting, wondering what he could want.

"Anyway, it took some maneuvering, but I was able to discover her friend. Curves, as I like to call her.

She hasn't had a boyfriend, isn't serious about anyone, and she's a virgin."

"How do you know that? They're in a city and could be screwing men every night," Gael said.

Just the thought of other men sniffing around our woman filled me with rage.

Earl smiled. "I have my means."

"You want Ashley?"

"Yes."

"Clearly something's going in here we're not privy to. Why don't you cut the crap and tell us what the deal is?"

Again, another smirk, which pissed me off. I didn't like to be at anyone's mercy and from the look of my friends, they didn't want to either. I was angry. I wanted to hurt someone, anyone.

"I give you Emily, and I'm taking Ashley. I want her indefinitely, which means I won't have you invading my time with her. She will belong to me. All of me. That is it. Simple."

"Hold on," Vadik said. "Let me get this straight. We get Emily, you have Ashley, and so long as we agree to leave you alone, we get our girl. No danger to her life."

"Exactly."

It was on the tip of my tongue to accept.

"We need to think about this," Gael said.

Now that did surprise me. Out of all of us, why would Gael want to think about this? I looked at him.

"Then, gentlemen, my offer lasts until the end of the evening, which is an hour away. I will go find myself something to eat. The kitchen is still this way?"

None of us went to stop him as he left the room.

Chapter Three

Gael

"How did that fucker make it from England to here?" River asked.

"Time-zone difference," I said. "Plus, he owns a private jet. It's not like he has to concern himself with canceled flights."

I ran a hand down my face, trying to clear my mind, which had fogged up from the moment Earl had entered our home. We all shared this place. The other three houses had been torn down and remained as ruins and reminders to all those who attempted to cross us.

I knew the nightmare we'd turned this place into. We'd created our own little playground. To a lot of people, our fathers' reign was filled with peace, while ours were riddled with terror.

"We are agreeing to this," Caleb said.

"I don't see what the deal is," River said. "We all want this."

Vadik agreed.

I was the fucked-up one. The mess. The person who struck first and asked questions later. After Emily had been taken from us, I'd been sent to get one of our minions. He was a bookkeeper, but he'd been investigated and found to be stealing from us. I'd stabbed him in the head, carried his body through the street, and when I dumped him in front of our fathers, they'd shouted questions at me. I'd grabbed him and used him as a puppet. It was the last time they had sent me to go find answers.

The pain of losing something so precious to me. It had stuck and I couldn't help it. Hurting people was my salvation.

I'd even hurt women. I'd lured them into my bed, taken their clothes, seen what dirty shit they wanted to do, filmed them, and destroyed them.

I hadn't slept with a woman. I hadn't allowed a woman to go down on me, nor to go anywhere near me. I know Caleb had. But I couldn't do it. River hadn't as well. Vadik kissed and teased, but I was the one who didn't go that far.

Staring at my friends now, my brothers in pain and pleasure, I couldn't believe I was the voice of reason. "Are you all fucking stupid?" I asked.

"Be careful," Caleb said.

I laughed. He'd broken my arm a couple of years ago during one of our many spars. The physical pain had been a welcome relief. It hadn't stopped me from starting fights.

"Emily is our woman and we know who she would protect with her life," I said. "If we give him Ashley, we will lose our woman."

"Not if we negotiate her life properly," River said.

I wanted Emily back, but I didn't want her to hate us. "If you make this deal with him, we will be fighting for her love."

"I don't care," Vadik said. "I need her back. We'll deal with the Ashley angle. She's had our girl for seven years. It's time we got her back, and if making a deal with that beast is what we've got to do, then so be it. We'll make it right eventually. Besides, Ashley owes us big time. I'm not going to talk about this. As far as I'm concerned, the deal has already been struck!"

He turned on his heel and left, Caleb following right after him, leaving me with River.

"I thought you were willing to do whatever it takes to get her back," River said.

I looked at him. He had several scars on his face. Some of them self-inflicted, others from fighting.

"I would."

"Then this is a done deal. Until we can find out a way to make it right, Emily will be ours."

He didn't give me chance to respond.

I stared at the man on the ground and tutted. "We're about to fuck up as badly as you. Hopefully, this time, she won't kill us." Whistling to myself, I followed my boys into the kitchen.

Earl had already started to eat his sandwich. "Damn good cheese you have here. I need to know your supplier."

"Cut the crap. Before we agree, we have a few conditions."

He burst out laughing. "You think you're in a position to be giving me conditions?" he asked.

"This isn't funny," Caleb said.

"I'm offering you the chance of a lifetime and this is all the thanks I get?" Earl rolled his eyes.

"You can't kill her," I said. This had to be number one for Ashley. If she was to die, it would kill Emily, I just knew it.

Earl chuckled. "I want to take her cherry not kill her."

"We know the games you play," Vadik said.

"No, you know the women I sell. I've never killed a woman."

"No one can kill her. Ashley has to stay alive."

"You know I can just take this girl."

"And we'd fight you because we'd do that for Emily," I said.

Earl looked at me. "I thought you were the crazy one."

"Emily loves her. They're still together even after

all this time. There is no fighting that."

He sighed. "I don't like this."

"It's the only arrangement we'll make," Caleb said.

Earl stared at us. Seconds passed.

"Fine. Ashley will stay alive. I have no plans to kill her. But, and this is the big but, you will entertain Emily while I get her. She belongs to me. I want time with her alone, away from prying eyes."

"Emily will want to see her." I had to make sure Emily got what she wanted.

Earl ran a hand down his face and shook his head. "I get six months with Ashley before any visiting."

"A month," I said.

Caleb sent me a sharp look. They clearly hadn't seen the connection between Emily and Ashley, but I had. I knew what was at stake. They could all take the credit, but I had to make sure she was taken care of.

"Not a chance. Five."

"Two."

"Four," Earl said.

I stared at him.

"Two, and you get to bring her here and leave when you want."

"Even if Ashley tries to convince you to let her go, you will make sure she leaves with me," Earl said.

"If she wants to leave you, then you should think about the women you keep," Caleb said.

"Deal," Earl said. "Now, I don't like to wait around. I want Ashley and I want her now. Let's go and fetch our women, boys."

****

Emily

"You're nervous," Ashley said.

We'd met up for coffee at a nice café. I'd decided to sit outside while she went to order for us. She returned with coffee and doughnuts. I nibbled on a piece of a doughnut, not really impressed with the texture of it in my mouth. It was a little cakey for my liking.

"I'm fine."

"Emily, stop lying to me. You think I haven't noticed the change in you? I have. I can see it, and I bet everyone else can as well. This isn't good for you."

I let out a sigh. "I'm sorry."

"Don't be sorry. Tell me what is wrong," she said.

When I was sure everyone around us wasn't assassins or Earl's buddies, I turned back to Ashley. "Do you ever get the sense you're being watched?"

"Is this some paranormal stuff? Like ghosts?"

"No, not like that."

"I need you to elaborate, Em."

"Like people are watching us. Familiar faces that are always there."

"We have work colleagues, and we've been living here for seven years. I'm sure we're going to experience that." She frowned. "I don't understand what the problem is."

I dropped my hands to the table, spreading out my fingers. "I don't know. Ugh. Ever since Earl came, I've felt it." I ran my fingers through my hair, feeling the hairs stand on end. There was also a twist in my gut I didn't like. Not one bit.

"What is it?" she asked.

"He came to warn me, and I don't know. Something feels off about this whole thing."

"You're starting to scare me," Ashley said. She took a long sip of her coffee and licked her fingers. "Your paranoia aside, I will be late tonight. I've got the late shift and also, Ronald has offered to show me how to make his Yorkshire puddings. I can't wait. Mine are always coming out so dry and flat."

I wrinkled my nose. "Really."

"Come on. I want to make everything perfect for Christmas dinner."

"We're months away."

"Nothing wrong with preparing in advance. Anyway, don't worry when I come in late."

"Oh, is this like a *date* date?"

"Ew, no. You do remember Ronald is married with three kids, right?"

"Right, yes, sorry."

"My mom may have been a cheater. I'm not one of them." Ashley sat back, her face pale.

"I'm sorry," I said. "I didn't mean to … insinuate."

"It's fine."

"It's not. This is all my fault." I felt bad now. I tried to never bring her mother up as it was full of bad memories. Her mother was a cheater, not that my father was any better. I reached across the table, taking her hands in mine. "I'm really sorry."

Ashley pulled away. "I need to get to work." She stood up and I watched her gather her bag.

"Ash, please, don't leave like this."

"I'm fine. I can forget for the most part, you know. She uprooted us, and I was more than happy to go along. I knew her man was married, and if it hadn't been for that, I wouldn't have met you."

"I'm really sorry."

"Doesn't change the fact she's dead. That they killed her." Her eyes glistened with tears. "I'll see you tomorrow."

I didn't get a chance to stop her. She moved too

fast, but I also knew she wanted to be alone, and I couldn't change that, nor could I blame her. Her only crime was having a mother who fell in love with my dad, who was a greedy bastard. The only saving grace we had was the fact he was dead as well. It didn't stop her from missing her mom. I hated this. There was absolutely nothing I could do. No way to console her.

Running my fingers through my hair, I got to my feet and paid for our coffees. There was no point in sticking around.

As I left the café, I glanced back, sure I'd seen someone I recognized. When I glanced over the tables, no one I knew was there. None of it made any sense to me. The feeling of being watched was still strong.

Rather than linger, I left, but I didn't go to work. I called the supermarket, claiming to be sick. Lying was second nature to me. With the unsettled feeling that rushed over me, I headed straight to my and Ashley's apartment. No one stopped me on my way, but I found myself stopping to look for anyone who could possibly be following me. It made no sense. Why would anyone wish to follow me? I was no one now, as Amelia.

I thought about Earl Valentine. I hadn't felt this way in a long time. My heart raced and I wished I had my knife with me. It had been a long time since I thought about having my knife. I thought back to the one River had taken. He'd never given it back to me after I killed that MC guy, stabbing him right through the neck. It felt like that had happened to someone else, not to me.

The way I felt was Earl's fault. If he hadn't turned up, I wouldn't be nervous or panicking. I'd be in control of all of my emotions, instead of being pissed off. While I rushed toward my apartment building, I stopped for the hundredth time and glanced out across the street. People were going about their business, completely oblivious to my craziness. Why would they even have to think about my life, or what I was going through? They had their own lives.

There was no one there. No one who stood out. I hated this feeling so fucking much.

Finally, I headed into my building, but I didn't take the elevator. I went for the stairs, running up them.

No one intercepted me.

As I grabbed my keys and went for my door, my hand shook. I didn't like how afraid I was. Gritting my teeth, I let myself inside my apartment, slamming the door closed and resting my palms against the wood.

My heart raced.

Someone was inside.

I knew they were.

My hands were hidden behind my body and I grabbed the keys, sliding one between my knuckles, ready to cause trouble.

I counted to ten inside my head, and then I turned, raising my hand, ready to take out whoever was in my place. They would regret coming here.

My wrist was caught and I cried out at the sudden pain, but I was pressed against the door, my hand lifted up. Then I was staring into a pair of blue eyes. I recognized them instantly. Gael Parson, in the flesh, had me trapped and as I stared at him, I was amazed. He was the same old Gael, and yet, he wasn't. He was darker, scarier. The part of him that always seemed to be joking, gone. No smile. No nothing.

Neither of us spoke.

I panted and he just stared. I released my keys and it seemed to shake him. In the next second, I threw my arms around him, taking possession of his lips.

Deep down, I knew I should be pissed at him, and I was. But I wasn't going to waste a moment. One of his hands sank into my hair as the other went to my ass. We both moaned as he pushed me back. This time, we missed the door and went straight for the wall. He broke off the kiss, sliding his lips down my neck to my pulse, and I moaned, wanting more.

Shoving against him, I pulled my bag over my head and let it go. It landed on the floor with a clatter, but I didn't care.

Next, I was back on him, and he lifted me as I wrapped my legs around his waist.

I wanted him so badly.

Gael and I, we never got to do this. I should be angry at him, telling him to fuck off, but with his hands wrapped around me, all I wanted was to feel him everywhere. We didn't get this chance before they pushed me away. I needed this.

My body craved his touch more than I wanted to push him away.

It was wrong. I knew that.

Afterward, I'd be pissed. I'd send him back to hell, but for now, I was going to be selfish and have this moment all to myself.

Gripping the edge of his shirt, I tore it open.

Buttons went flying in either direction. I caught sight of all of his ink, the old mixed with the new, but I didn't care.

We moved to my sofa and he dropped me down.

It was a battle of wills, getting each other naked. I didn't know exactly who won as we both ended up without our clothes, and that was more than fine with me. Our clothes were on the floor all around us and I stared at him, waiting.

"Fuck, I forgot how beautiful you are."

I didn't hide. I held myself still, watching him, waiting. He just kept looking at me and I liked it.

I hadn't been with anyone else, nor had I dated. I didn't want anyone else but him, along with his three other friends. I didn't care if it was conventional. They hadn't left me alone. They all promised me forever, and instead, I had a mere taste of what it meant to be owned by the Monsters' Crew before they discarded me.

The pain shook me to my core, but rather than dwell, I stared at him for a few seconds and then sank to my knees before him. Wrapping my fingers around his length, I worked him up and down.

His fingers went to my hair, holding on to the strands. Staring up the length of his body, I flicked the tip of his cock with my tongue. The growl that erupted from his lips sent a thrill down my spine. I liked that I can do this to him. I didn't take him into my mouth immediately. No, I took my sweet time, torturing him, making him wait. I didn't want him to get off easily.

Sliding my tongue down the vein, I watched him close his eyes for a split second before they were back on me. Good. I wanted him to know who was doing this to him. I didn't know if he'd had other women, and I didn't want to know right now. All I was interested in was what I could get out of this.

None of the other women mattered.

When I'd coated him in my saliva and made him wait enough, I took him into my mouth, covering the entire tip. Up and down, I bobbed on him, relishing the sounds he made as he hit the back of my throat. I almost gagged on the length with how big he was.

He held my head and moved me up and down his length, and I took him, loving every single second of his touch. Even the force as he made me take him. At a few points, I gagged, but within a matter of seconds, he pushed me off his length.

Gael sat me on the edge of the sofa, moving me

back, and then his tongue danced across my pussy. His tongue sliding through my slit, circling my clit, then down to my entrance. I cried out as he fucked inside me, and the pleasure was instant.

I'd touched myself, but none of it felt like this. Gael's tongue was working his magic and all it took were a few strokes, and I was coming. I screamed his name, but I didn't want him to stop. He didn't. He was licking and sucking at my pussy as if I was the food he'd been dying to eat, and I loved it.

I begged him to not stop, and he hurtled me into a second orgasm that shocked me with just how quickly he got me off. I wasn't used to coming so fast, but that was what he did to me.

My body was sated and I waited. Gael sat back, wiping his face with his palm, and then he was back between my thighs. The hard length of his cock rubbing between my lips. Each time he hit my clit, I arched up, and his hands went from my hips, up to my tits, squeezing them.

"So fucking hot." He moved down.

I looked at him as I felt the tip against my core.

In one hard thrust, he slammed deep inside and we both cried out.

His grip on my tits didn't let up. He held them and started to pound inside me, going deeper as he filled me. I heard the sounds of just how wet I was as he started to fuck me. Going in deep, pulling out.

"So pretty. Do you have any idea how many times I've been wanting to fuck you? To drive my dick inside you? I've thought about it every single day."

"Shut up and fuck me," I said. The last thing I wanted to hear was what he'd been craving or doing while I'd been away. He'd left me. He'd fucking left and I didn't want to have to deal with that. Asshole. He

45

pissed me off by even thinking I wanted to hear what he went through.

He released my tits, grabbed my hips, and started to pound inside me.

I wasn't used to the sheer width and size of him, and it took my breath away with just how fucking hard he was.

He pistoned in me, not letting up, and I didn't want him to stop. I screamed his name, desperate for more. Hungry for him.

Gael gave me what I wanted and as I came on his length, he cried out, his hard cock filling me with his cum. We didn't use any protection. I didn't say anything as I came down from my high.

His dick was still inside me. I stared at him, wondering if these feelings he inspired would ever dissipate. I was so angry, at myself and at him. I wanted to scream.

"Hello, Emily," he said.

There was a twinkle in his eye, as well as a smirk. I was super pissed and I reacted. After drawing my fist back, I clocked him in the face. He reeled back, pulling out of me. I stood up, feeling his cum sliding out of me, down my thigh, but I didn't care. Not at that moment. I glared at him and then stomped away.

I just couldn't bring myself to say how much I hated, loved, and needed him at that moment. Instead, I went for a shower. It was the only thing that felt safe to me right now. Everything else, my feelings, they were too much. I was drowning in them and that wasn't a good feeling. It was a bad one. I needed to get my shit together before I completely lost it.

Chapter Four

Caleb

As we stepped into Emily and Ashley's apartment, I caught sight of Gael putting his clothes on.

"You couldn't wait?" River asked.

"It's easy for you to say. You're not the one who's had to wait all this time. You've had a taste of her." Gael stepped into his pants.

"I had one taste."

Gael and I didn't get a chance with Emily before our fathers interfered. To a point, it had put a strain on our friendship with River and Vadik, especially when we were drunk and our anger reached a new kind of high.

Much to my surprise, neither River nor Vadik minded. They seemed to get that we'd missed out on her.

"Where is she?" I asked. I don't want to reminisce about the past. There was no point. All I wanted was to see our woman. We'd been too long without and we'd made a deal with the fucking devil to get her back. Before she could realize what we'd done, we needed to get her home. Not that Crude Hill could be called home.

The moment Ashley didn't come home tonight, she'd realize we sacrificed her best friend in order to claim her. We'd deal with the fallout so long as we had a chance to chain her to us in every single way that mattered.

I didn't trust Earl one bit, and that was another reason I wanted Emily back in our town. Once we had her within our protective circle, she would be safe.

"You need to leave," Emily said.

She was completely wet. Her hair fell down around her shoulders and she had a towel wrapped around her body. She hadn't looked up at us, and just seeing her now, my cock went so hard. She'd lost weight, which I didn't like.

We'd take care of her.

Seconds ticked by, and she looked up, coming to a stop.

"Fuck me," she said.

All four of us were in her apartment, which was so tiny compared to our place back home.

Her gaze moved over all of us until she finally settled on me.

"What is this?" She stayed perfectly still.

"It's time for you to come home," I said.

Her hands went left to right. "No, I am home."

"This isn't your home," Gael said. "You know it. I know it."

"I don't have to listen to this. You had your fun."

Her glare was so fucking cute.

Gael chuckled. "I seem to recall you had your fun just as much. You used me to scratch that itch of yours."

"You think you're funny?"

"Hilarious."

She rolled her eyes and it was so good to watch her. I'd missed this.

"You can all leave." Her teeth sank into her lip and I caught the glistening of her eyes. It cut me deeply to know we were the ones responsible for the way she felt. We'd hurt her. No one else.

It made me want to beat the shit out of myself, but I couldn't do that. "Em, you've got to come with us."

She burst out laughing. "You're all joking. Not happening. You need to leave. With Earl's appearance, Ashley's already having a hard time dealing with everything. Unlike us, she loved her mom."

"We've got Ashley," I said. I was going straight

to hell for the lies that spilled from my lips. "Do you think we'd risk coming here if it wasn't important? You and Ashley are in danger. We've already got Ashley on the way back to Crude Hill. Your lives are in danger."

"You're lying. Ashley told me you sent me here for my own good."

"Yes, and she didn't lie, but things change, Emily. You know this life better than anyone. We're not going to let anything happen to you." She was going to hate me, but so long as I got her ass back in Crude Hill, in our home, I didn't care.

Her gaze left mine and she looked toward Vadik, River, and Gael. I hoped they kept straight fucking faces.

I was doing what I needed to in order to get her home.

"Ashley's safe?"

"Yes."

"I need to call her." She moved as if to go and see, and I reacted. Wrapping my arms around her, we were going for plan B. I didn't want this one, but she was too damn stubborn. River was there with the needle, and he pressed it into her skin. "What the hell are you doing? Let me go. Let me the fuck go."

She was no match for my strength. I held her as the sedative took effect. Her grip on the towel loosened and it dropped to the floor. I kept my arms around her as she slumped in my arms.

I looked toward Gael. "Get her some clothes."

"Since when did I become your servant?"

"Just get her some fucking clothes." I didn't have time to argue. The moment the sedative went into her, we were on a countdown. We only had one other dose and I didn't want to waste time.

The sooner we got her to Crude Hill, the better.

Vadik and River watched me. I hadn't let her go.

"You lied to her," River said.

"You think she was going to come with us?" I didn't know why I was trying to justify myself to them.

"I don't know, but lying to her wasn't exactly ideal, was it?" Vadik asked. "She's going to know the truth now, and we're going to have to fight her."

"If she knows what's good for her, she'll do as she's told." I sounded like an asshole, but I didn't care. I was trying to keep her safe, protect her.

Gael returned with a pair of sweats and an ugly-ass t-shirt with a cat on it. Kind of strange for Emily, but I didn't care. With Gael's help, we got her changed and I lifted her in my arms.

"Wait," Gael said, stopping me as I walk toward the door.

"What?"

"You think we should, you know, grab a few things for her?"

"We're about to have a fight for our life in keeping her. Do you really fucking think this is going to help us if she has any memories of all that we've taken from her?" I was losing my temper now.

"It may help," Vadik said.

"If you guys want to stay behind and grab sentimental shit, be my guest. I don't have time." I worked the door open and left, carrying the love of our life with me down toward our waiting car.

****

Vadik

Emily hadn't woken up yet.

We were on our plane, heading to the airport, where a car was waiting for us to escort us all back to Crude Hill.

I couldn't take my eyes off her.

We'd lain down her seat and she was curled up. River threw a blanket on her, and she looked so perfect. Peaceful within sleep but also because we finally had her back.

Caleb sat beside her, drinking some whiskey. I noticed his hands shook a little, but I didn't comment. He wasn't afraid. None of us were. With the life we'd lived these past few years, fear wasn't easy to come by.

Emily, though, she was finally with us, and Earl had come through. Ashley was gone and she was still alive.

We'd fucked up. I knew we had.

Gael sat a couple of seats down from me, staring at her. He'd finally tasted her, and I knew what he was going through. The pleasure that rushed through you, the feel of her wrapped around you. I'd had a chance to experience it once myself, but since then, nothing else.

I missed it.

I missed that feeling.

Seeing her now, I was overcome by guilt. There had been women over the years, some I'd tried to use to make me forget her. I'd never gone all the way with them, but the intent had been there.

Earl had given us a chance to look into Emily's past. There wasn't anyone. Her life was dull. She worked constantly. Ashley had more fun than our girl. I didn't like it. Emily was supposed to live a full and happy life, not to sit around waiting for us.

I couldn't help but be happy no man had stolen her from us. We would've killed anyone who dared to take her away from us.

"She's going to hate us," Gael said. "The moment she realizes what we've done."

"She won't find out straight away." Caleb sipped at his whiskey while staring out the window. He always claimed to be in control but I knew different. He was holding on by a thread. Out of all four of us, he was now the only one not to know how perfect she felt on your cock.

"No? You think the way we reacted she wasn't put on the alert? Emily isn't stupid," Gael said, standing.

"Sit down. I'm very much aware of who she is and what she's capable of. What I'm telling you is she won't learn the truth from me. We'll keep her in the dark until we can't."

"You think that's wise?" River asked.

"I'm doing what is best for her."

"How do we know Earl is even going to keep his word?" I asked, lifting my gaze to them.

All of them looked at me as if I was stupid.

"Sure, we got her and so far nothing bad has happened, but it doesn't mean Earl will keep his word."

"He'll keep his word," Caleb said.

"Why? Yeah, we're all deadly and scary, but why does he have to? He lives by his own rules."

"Don't forget the full agreement. He's going to be sticking around," Caleb said.

"I think we're being stupid if we trust him." I ran a hand down my face. The last twenty-four hours were catching up to me. Traveling to England and back again, finding Emily, it was all starting to mount up. It wouldn't be long before I was literally asleep standing up. It wouldn't be the first time I'd gone without sleep.

We'd all suffered to get to where we are now.

"One problem at a time," Caleb said. "That's all we can do."

As if on cue, Emily started to stir. She let out a moan. Her body was slow as she came to. We all tensed. None of us knew what was going to happen.

River had the needle ready in case she started to

lose it.

Caleb held his hand up, putting his whiskey down. "Emily, baby."

Her eyes opened, those intense green emeralds that captured my fucking soul. One look into them, and I knew we were about to have an explosion. Before she got a chance to, River was there, injecting her.

This was the final countdown.

Caleb stepped back.

"Well, we always did admire her spirit," River said. "I guess we're about to find the real fire that makes our woman."

"She'll come around," Caleb said.

"You keep saying that. Are you trying to convince yourself or us?" I asked.

He glared at me. "I see you're happy with pointing fingers but never making a full-blown decision. You don't like this, why didn't you speak up?"

"I don't like it, but I also see it's the only way. What I'm trying to get you to see, Caleb, is that this isn't going to be easy. Emily isn't going to be easily wowed. I imagine when she wakes up, she's going to be plotting our deaths."

"I don't mind so long as she's with us," Gael said. "We've already lost so much time. I always felt we were fucking pussies for not going to get her."

"We weren't pussies," I said. "We were keeping her alive."

"And what about now?" Gael asked. "We're taking her to where our fathers live."

"Yeah, but they're not the Monsters anymore," Caleb said. "We are."

That was what we'd become.

I stared at Emily. Her face had lost the frown, but I knew it was just the drugs. If we weren't careful, we were going to lose her, and I couldn't allow that to happen.

****

River

We got her home.

The sedative worked until we got her in the driveway. We'd been fucking blessed to get her this far, but she turned into a hellcat.

She kneed me in the balls, clocked Gael in the jaw, and bit onto Caleb's arm. When she tried to run, I pushed through the pain and rushed toward her. We both went down and I made sure I was the one to suffer rather than her.

I had her arms by her sides, hoping she wouldn't stop me from being able to father children. She wriggled, screamed curses. This wasn't going to look good in front of our men. Caleb got to her first and I saw she'd drawn blood on his arm. Not too much but enough. He somehow had grabbed some rope or it had been stored close, I didn't know how.

"Let me go. Let me go right now." She screamed.

I noticed not once did she beg for anyone to help her. I didn't know if that was because she knew we wouldn't hurt her or if she figured it was a lost cause.

None of our men would interfere.

This wasn't good, though.

With Gael close, I let go of her arms and put my hand across her mouth. Instantly, she tried to bite me, but I was able to avoid those vicious teeth.

Gael and Vadik helped as Caleb used his expertise and wrapped that rope around her wrists. Her feet were still a problem. Caleb hauled her over his shoulder. Gael offered me a hand.

I made sure to look at all the men who'd

witnessed the scene before them. If they knew what was good for them, they'd turn a-fucking-way. Part of me wanted them to test us now, to try to take one of us out.

No one did.

They all turned away as if they hadn't seen anything.

We didn't hire cowards and the men here were loyal and even still, it pissed me off.

Following Caleb and a wriggling, curse-spewing Emily into our home, I wasn't shocked when he took her straight upstairs, going to one of our guest bedrooms. It made me smile when I saw he'd picked the one with a four-poster bed. The things we could do to her just by tying her up. It would be a whole lot of fun.

He dumped her on the bed and tied the rope around the board, knotting it up.

"You think this is funny?" she asked.

"What I'm doing is for your own good." He snarled at her.

"Well, look at you, you taking charge. Where's your daddy? Don't you need to go and kiss his arse?" The way she spoke now had an English twang to her words, and it was so fucking sexy.

Caleb fisted some of her hair. "I don't need my daddy. I'm the one in charge. You're at our mercy, Emily. So, it's about time you start playing nice with us."

"I have played nice. Ask Gael. I'm sure you already know about River and Vadik. Just you left, and guess what, I'm not going to be giving you anything." She tried to pull away but his grip kept her immobile. They were both panting and just watching them made my cock hard.

I'd missed her fire, her passion, her mouth. The times we'd shared when we were younger, they hadn't been enough. I couldn't stop looking at her.

"Oh, you will, Emily. You're going to give me everything and what's more, you're going to beg me for it."

"Think again."

"No? Put it this way, unless you start to learn to play nice, you're never going to see your friend again." Caleb slammed his lips down on hers as I turned to look at Gael and Vadik for any idea what he was fucking doing.

Of course, we didn't give anything away.

Caleb pulled away.

"River, let me out," she said. Her lips were swollen and her cheeks flushed.

I shook my head and turned on my heel.

Next, she called Vadik and then Gael. All of us left, not getting involved. Caleb closed the door, flicking the lock into place.

"You want to tell us what that was all about?" I asked.

"I need a drink."

"You had plenty on the plane." We all had our vices, but we'd made sure not one of us succumbed to the addiction. For now, it had been easy, but that didn't mean it couldn't change. I stared at him, waiting.

Caleb looked at me. "Don't for a second think you can tell me what to do. I need a drink, sleep, and then I'll deal with the wildcat. Until then, stay out of my fucking face."

He pushed away from us and I let him go. We were all tense, and I couldn't say I blamed him.

"I'm out," Gael said. Before he left, he put his palm flat against the wood of the door. "She's finally home where she's supposed to be."

It was the first time he'd looked at peace.

With him gone, it left me and Vadik.

"What are your thoughts on this?" I asked.

Vadik looked at the door. "She's home. That's all we need."

He left me alone. Probably to go and draw another picture for his constant shrine to her. He'd have plenty of inspiration today.

Me, I looked at the door. I didn't want to leave, but I also couldn't face her yet. I wasn't ready.

I didn't know what Caleb's game was, but I had to be in control and ready for whatever he planned to dish out. It was going to get messy. I knew it was, deep down in my soul.

We'd stolen Emily, bargained her friend's life, and we could have just handed her a death sentence. I didn't trust Earl Valentine, but for now, I intended to just get some sleep. It was all I could do.

****

Caleb

Sleep wasn't as easy to come by as I thought it would be, which pissed me off. After how long I'd been up, you'd think I would be able to just hit the pillow and be out for the count. Not even a little bit, which pissed me off.

Running a hand down my face, I stood outside Emily's door.

I'd gotten the cook and a couple of housekeepers to go to her, but they'd come back covered in soup, along with bite marks.

The one on my arm still felt good to me. I enjoyed the pain. It showed she still had feelings for us, even if she did try to hide it. There was no getting away from what we were to each other.

In my hand, I held a bag of chips and a sandwich. Opening the door, I found Emily sitting on the bedroom floor, her hands clasped together. She tilted her head back and looked at me.

The anger was still there.

I closed the door and moved toward her. Sitting within touching distance, I expected her to lash out, but she didn't.

"You're going to play nice."

"Fuck you, Caleb."

I smiled. "Good to know you're not giving in."

She pressed her lips together.

"You certainly hurt those two girls. They were just doing their job."

She looked at me. "Are they okay?"

"They'll live. I'll make sure to give them a bonus for dealing with you."

"Aren't you nice."

"I'm the best." When I held up the sandwich for her to eat, she shook her head. "You've got to eat something. You've lost too much weight and I don't like it."

"Why didn't you just leave me there?"

"Not going to happen. You knew we were coming for you."

"Bullshit. I didn't know you were coming for me. You bargained my life, all of you did."

"To save you."

She took a deep breath.

"If you try to starve yourself, that's fine. I don't mind if you make this difficult. I'll do whatever it takes to keep you healthy. You know that, so why don't you cut the crap and save us both the hassle?"

"I don't like you."

"Yeah, you do. It's why you're behaving this way. Don't worry. I won't hold it against you." I waited, as did she, but like I knew she would, she took a bite of the sandwich. "See, not so bad."

"What did you do to Ashley?" she asked after chewing and swallowing.

"You're going to have to eat the whole sandwich before I tell you a thing."

"I don't like this, Caleb. You think I don't know how this works? I saw Earl. I talked to him. He's part of this," she said.

Fuck. I didn't want to tell her any of the details too soon, but she knew everything about our life. She'd been part of it and lived it herself.

"Eat."

"Damn it, Caleb."

"Eat. That's all you're going to get from me."

"This isn't fair."

"No, you know what isn't fair, it's living your life for the past seven years wondering about you, wanting you, craving you, but not being able to do a damn thing about it because of what your parents threatened. You think none of us wanted you? You think we didn't regret trying to save you?" I needed her to understand.

She finished chewing her next mouthful of food. "I don't want to talk about this."

"Emily!"

"No, don't Emily me. You talk about how bad it has been for you, what about me? I was the one whose life was in the balance. Me and Ashley." She stopped, pressing her lips together. "You know I've hated you all for so long. I even went through a stage of wishing I hadn't saved Gael. None of this would have happened. You wouldn't have gotten me to love you, or to care—"

I silenced the rest of her tirade with a kiss. She froze beneath my touch, not making a sound, not even giving me a chance. I wasn't going to give up easily. She wanted my kisses, I just knew it.

If Emily no longer wanted me, us, she would have moved on already. There would already be a man waiting in the wings, but there wasn't. She was alone and that told me she'd been waiting a long time, pinning for me, for us.

The instant she responded felt glorious. Her tongue traced against mine. From a dull kiss, it turned into a fire I didn't want to extinguish. She was so fucking good, so hot, so everything. I couldn't get enough of her.

Suddenly, she jerked back. "This doesn't change anything."

"About you hating us?" I chuckled when she didn't even nod or give me anything else. "I'm used to people hating us. You can hate me because I know right now your pussy is soaking wet and probably still has traces of Gael's cum inside you. You want us and for now, that's fine with me." I picked up the other half of the sandwich and offered it to her. "You can keep being stubborn all you want. Eventually, you'll wear yourself out, and it will be up to us to pick up the pieces. It's your decision."

She still glared at me but took the sandwich and began to eat. I didn't like binding her hands up, but for now, it was going to have to be a necessity.

"What did you do to Ashley?" she asked.

"Nothing."

"Don't lie to me, Caleb."

I didn't answer her right away. She was everything I ever wanted and now that I had her, I didn't want to give her up. Even if Earl hadn't come through, I was going to move heaven and earth to make sure she could stay part of us.

Chapter Five

Emily

Before Caleb left me alone last night, he gave me enough room to be able to sleep. He hadn't allowed me total freedom and now as I stood, dancing around the bed, I was so fucking pissed.

I needed to use the bathroom, like desperately, and so far, no one had arrived. Gripping the pole of the bed, I rested my forehead against the hard wood, breathing in and out, trying to calm my need that was only increasing as the seconds passed.

This wasn't funny.

I knew without a doubt they'd made a deal or done something that involved Ashley, I just couldn't figure out what.

Right now, my brain wasn't working. I couldn't figure anything out. Everything felt like too much. My focus just wasn't working. In and out, I tried to breathe, not to panic or freak out.

All I could do was keep on moving. Pressing my thighs together and attempting to think about everything and nothing that would keep me from soiling myself. This wasn't the plan I had for today.

Attacking the guys had been a big mistake, but my anger had gotten the better of me, along with my pain. They'd left me and now that they'd deemed it safe, they were back as if nothing bad had happened, and it pissed me off. They couldn't just go in and out of my life like they had no care in the world. I didn't accept it, but right now, I'd give anything for one of them to walk right into this room and to help me out of this fucking rope.

Time ticked by and when I thought it would be too late, the door opened, showing River. He stood holding a knife. His chest rising and falling as if he'd been for a run.

"About time. Come on, please, I need to pee." I hated that I even asked him politely, but right now, I'd do just about anything.

I wasn't afraid as he came toward me. He lifted the knife and sliced through the rope with ease.

Rushing to the first door, I found a closet, but the next door was the trophy. A bathroom. I slammed the door closed and rushed toward the toilet, pushing down the sweats as I sat down.

Of course, my peace didn't last long as River walked right into the room.

"Please, some privacy."

"I'm here to make sure you wash up."

"You've cut the rope. Surely, you can trust me."

He smiled, but it wasn't a charming, sweet look on him. It was almost deadly. River had always had a darker edge around him. It was always like he was on the brink of danger, of waiting for the anger to seep into every single part of his soul. When he was young, he'd been taken, tortured, and because of that, he had an overwhelming obsession with blades, like now. He still held the blade as if it was a lifeline.

Taking a closer look at the blade, I was surprised to see that it was in fact the knife I once had, the one I'd embedded into an MC's neck to save Gael.

"You didn't get rid of it?"

"Why would I get rid of anything that reminded me of you?"

"I don't know." I didn't want to think. After I finished on the toilet, my face on fire for having him listen, I went to the sink and washed my hands. "What's going on, River?"

He stayed in front of the door. "You're going to

take a bath. I'm going to make sure you don't do something you'll regret."

"So, you're my own personal bodyguard."

"From this day forward, you're going to have one of us at your beck and call."

Turning toward the bathtub, I frowned. "My beck and call? You mean you're going to keep me here to protect me?"

"Let's just say we're taking care of our investment."

This made me stand up. "Just tell me what the hell you did. What you agreed to?" I needed to know. I just knew I wasn't going to like any of it, but still, I had to find out what stupid thing they'd done.

He stayed perfectly still, his gaze running up and down my body. In the sweats, I must have looked a sight, and I checked to make sure I didn't embarrass myself with my overwhelming need for the toilet. There was nothing there.

"Why do you keep staring?" I asked.

When the bath had enough bubbles and water, I turned toward him.

"You're not going to talk to me? You're just going to ignore me?" I gripped the edge of the shirt and lifted it up and over my head. My guys hadn't bothered to give me underwear, so I was completely naked beneath.

I didn't wait for a reaction and kicked off my sweats. When I bent over to test the water, I did hear a groan, and I couldn't help but smile. He could act all unaffected by me all he wanted, but I knew the truth. He wanted me and I was more than okay with that.

I hated my men, but that didn't mean I also didn't want them all with an equal passion. It was complicated. I didn't understand my own feelings when it came to these men. They were not boys anymore; no, they'd ever been boys.

Sitting in the water, I leaned back, resting myself against the tub so I could look at him. "See, I'm doing as I'm told."

"You and I both know you're not going to do as you're told."

I chuckled. "I try."

"No, you don't. Not anymore. We made sure you didn't have to worry about anyone or anything. You're free."

"You call this free?" I asked. "You took me from my home, and now you're keeping me hostage."

"We're not keeping you hostage. We're not bargaining you for anything."

I took a deep breath. Sliding beneath the water, I soaked my hair and broke the surface again, lifting out and reaching for the soap, but it was already gone.

River had it in his hand, and he'd put the blade on the side of the tub. I didn't know why he'd done that. Was it to test me? To see what I'd do? My heart raced as I stared at the damn thing.

"Go ahead," River said. "Take it."

"No."

This time, his laughter sent a thrill down my spine. Looking up at him, I saw he no longer looked like he wanted to kill. There was a playfulness about him. "Are you just going to keep doing the complete opposite of what we want you to do?"

"Is that a problem?"

"Not to me, but the others might start to get pissed off."

I took a deep breath, trying to convince myself that I didn't care, but I did.

Gripping the edge of the blade, I picked it up. In

my mind, I recalled how it felt sliding into the MC's neck. I licked my lips and wondered what the hell to do.

"It feels good, doesn't it?"

I went to put the blade down, but River stopped me. His hand covered mine, holding it.

"River?"

"I'm not going to hurt you. You should know that by now." His grip was tight but not to the point of pain. "Do you have any idea how many people I've killed with this?"

I looked up to find him staring down at me, waiting for me to answer. There were no words. No way of telling or asking him what he means. Instead, I held on to the knife like it was a lifeline, waiting.

"You've used this to kill people?"

"Yes, a lot of people deserve to die, and I just can't resist hurting people. You of all people should know that by now, Emily." He sighed. "I keep this on me at all times."

"Why?"

"You know why."

"River, I'm not sure what's going on here."

"You get it. I know you do."

"I'm not going to hurt you," I said.

"I know."

He took the blade from me and placed it on the floor. I was a little confused but that was soon replaced when he started to clean my body. He'd soaped up a sponge and now he was so very gentle with me. With the short-sleeved shirt he wore, I saw all the new lines of scars. Knife wounds, which I reached out and touched. Sliding my finger across each edge, feeling a little taken aback.

There was fresh ink there as well, but I could pick out the problems.

His breath fanned against my ear. "Do you have any idea how close I've come to death?"

This made me pull away. I instantly went to my knees and captured his face. "Why?" I didn't like how upset I was. It meant these men affected me deeply. They always said there was a fine line between love and hate, and right now, I struggled with every part of it. I felt a little sick to my stomach.

"What do you mean, why?" he asked.

"Is it to punish me?"

"Emily, you're not making any sense."

"Why would you put yourself in danger?" I asked. I wanted to slap him, but I wouldn't give him the satisfaction.

"You know who we are, what we are. We don't have a choice. It's kill or be killed. It doesn't mean they don't get a shot in. We're still alive, just a little more cut up than you're used to." He lifted a finger and pushed some of my wet hair out of my face. "But even while you hate us, it's good to know you don't wish me dead."

"I don't want you to die. I want you to tell me the truth of what the hell is going on. You sent me on my merry way seven years ago, and now you're back. Don't think I don't know what that means. Deals have to be made and I'm part of them. Why?"

"I'm not saying a thing to you."

"Is this because of Caleb? Is he the one completely in charge now?" I asked.

River's gaze was still on me like he could see right through me. "You can try to anger me all you want, it doesn't change anything. We're a team and the only reason I'm not going to say anything to you, Emily, is because we're all going to be telling you what is going on."

Before I knew what was happening, he gripped

my head and dunked me underneath the water. I came up spluttering while River looked calm and relaxed as if he didn't have a care in the world.

It must be nice to be him.

I glared at him but refused to assist him. He didn't seem to mind. In fact, he was more than happy to let me be still as he washed my body, my hair. When he was done, he stood with a towel.

The child in me wanted to throw water at him. Instead, I stood and held my arms out, waiting.

I let out a little yelp when he lifted me straight from the water without any problem at all. I was shocked, but River dropped the towel, cupped my face, and took my lips in a possessive kiss that thrilled me right down to my toes.

He was the first to break the kiss and I noticed how he rearranged his cock. He took my hand and led me right back into the bedroom where I found we'd had a delivery. Clothes, shoes, and the entire bedroom had been converted into something that resembled my room back in England.

I also noticed a picture on the nightstand, and I let go of River to pick it up. It was of me and Ashley. As always, my best friend was smiling, while I was pretending to be happy. I'd give anything to know she was okay. I didn't like to think of her as being alone with no one to come home to.

Holding the picture, I turned toward River. "Tell me she's safe."

"She's safe."

He said the words I wanted to hear, but I couldn't help but wonder if he'd just lied to me.

****

River

I drew the short straw.

Caleb had said he wanted Emily protected and we all knew the reason. Earl had gone quiet on us. We knew from our sources that he'd already taken Ashley and the apartment they had once shared had been completely cleared out as if the two girls didn't exist. But, and this was way out there, he hadn't gone to the house we'd negotiated for him. In fact, Earl was gone, disappeared, taking our bargaining chip with him.

"Breakfast or a walk outside?" I asked as Emily came out of the bathroom dressed in a pair of jeans and a long shirt that molded around her breasts but flared out and rested against her knees.

"What?"

"I'm going to have to do something about your manners." I chuckled. "Do you want to go for a walk first or would you like some breakfast?"

She looked toward the window. It was slightly overcast. Not the perfect walking weather.

"Outside first."

I nodded and held my arm up for her to take. I wasn't surprised when she looked at my offering as if it was going to spook her. "No strings attached. I'm with you today."

"You weren't this attentive years ago."

"Then consider yourself lucky."

I expected her to keep on arguing but instead, she took my arm without another word. I was shocked, but I didn't show it.

While I was babysitting Emily, which I loved, Gael, Vadik, and Caleb were putting our men back in their place, making them aware of their loyalty. If news got out of Emily's return, they would have to deal with us. There would be some death today. I had no doubt we had enemies within our soldiers, but we had no problem picking them off one by one.

I walked Emily down to the main floor and moved toward the second dining room that led out toward the garden. We passed several of our guards, all of whom averted their gaze, refusing to look at our woman. Good.

Emily stopped at the steps leading down toward the pristine mowed lawn. She took a deep breath.

I waited for her to take the next step, which she did, putting one foot in front of the other as we made our way to the grass. She bent down, removing the sneakers she'd picked along with the socks. I clicked my fingers, having one of our men take her shoes.

"Really?" she asked. "You've got people to do everything?"

"We pay them to be whatever we need."

"Must be nice."

I stayed silent. We'd gone out of our way to instill fear into our men. No one messed with us.

Emily sighed. "While you were taking over Crude Hill, I was working my ass off."

"Your apartment was fully paid for," I said. It was one of the reasons we were pissed off. Our money paid for the women, but it seemed with a snap of his fingers, Earl had been able to take that from us as well.

When we got to Earl, his body would fertilize the ground. I was sure of it. If he did anything to Ashley, Emily would never forgive us.

I imagined it was why Caleb had most of our contacts and spies hunting for him. The problem with Earl was that he was a ghost. No one could find him unless he wanted to be found.

"Yes, it was paid for." She chuckled. "We had no idea what to do. For the first month, we didn't even leave the apartment. There was enough food to feed an army.

Ashley's a damn good cook." She sighed. "We got by. I don't know how we did it. Eventually, leaving and visiting the city, it was easy to do, and got easier."

"What were you expecting?"

"I don't know. To be killed at a moment's notice." She pushed some hair out of her way. "What have you done to her?"

"She's fine."

"I don't like not knowing where my friend is. Ashley never did anything wrong."

"Em, what makes you think she's in danger?"

She pulled out of my hold and spread her arms wide. "Look around you." Gone was the reserved woman I recalled from high school. She'd lost that control. The woman before me was more open, more passionate, and I fucking loved it. "I know the deal that was made, River. What changed? Your parents aren't in control anymore and from what little information Earl gave, they hadn't been for a lot longer than now." She folded her arms. "Tell me."

"I can't tell you."

She stamped her foot.

"Ashley was the price," Caleb said, surprising the both of us.

I turned to see Gael, Vadik, and of course Caleb on the steps leading toward where we stood.

"What?" Emily asked.

"Earl came to us. He knew your location and how to keep you safe."

She burst out laughing. "Let me get this straight, you made a deal with a man who was willing to pay millions for a virg…" She stopped talking and looked at all of us while shaking her head. "No. Tell me no. Tell me you didn't bargain my best friend's virginity on this man to get me back."

"It wasn't just to get you back," Gael said.

"He offered to help out with what our fathers had done. The arrangement he'd made to keep you away from Crude Hill."

Tears were in her eyes. "You're all fools," she said. "He wants what he feels was taken from him, doesn't he?"

None of us confirmed her assumptions. There was no reason to. She already knew the truth.

"Where's Ashley? Tell me you got her before he could put his hands on her."

None of us spoke.

Emily turned away and started to pace. "Where is she?"

"We don't know that," Vadik said.

Caleb held his hand up as if to stop him from talking. "No, I'm not going to keep this shit from her. We fucked up. We made a deal and jumped in because we only saw what we wanted. This is our mess. This is on us, not on her. This is our fault."

"What's happened?" Emily asked.

Caleb sighed. "Earl Valentine has gone missing, along with your friend. We don't know if he has stuck to his arrangement or if he's made a fool out of us."

This, for some reason, had Emily laughing. It was more on the hysterical side. "You've got to be kidding me, right?"

None of us laughed.

This made her stop and look at us. She pressed her lips together. "She's innocent."

Again, there was nothing we could say to make her feel any better. We'd fucked up, we all knew that.

She turned on her heel and started toward the stairs. I followed her; however, Caleb reached out, capturing her waist.

Emily slapped him hard and fast right across the face.

The guards came forward, guns raised, and Caleb held up his hand to stop them.

"I hate you," she said. "She is better than all of us. She's kind, good, and sweet, and you sold her as if she was worth nothing."

"You're worth everything."

"Not compared to her. I promised myself she would be free. She'd know only happiness."

"We're going to find her."

I knew Caleb was talking out of his ass. There was no way we could find her, otherwise, we'd have done it already.

"Good, I want her back and now." Emily stormed away, and I had no choice but to follow close behind her.

She entered the house and made wet footprints across the carpet until we got to the hallway.

She put her hand on the door and stopped.

"You can't leave," I said. "You're no good to her dead."

"I can't believe you'd be stupid enough to make a deal with that man." She turned accusing eyes at me.

I nodded for the soldier who was close to the door to leave. Grabbing Emily's arm, I marched her into the room we used as an office, slamming the door closed and shoving her up against it.

"I get that you're fucking upset, but you need to start being careful about what you say to us and when."

"Bite me!"

Sinking my fingers into her hair, I pulled her close to me, and I just couldn't help it, I took her lips. Biting down onto the plump flesh, I heard her moan. After plunging my tongue into her mouth, I traced across her lips, tasting her. My cock was already rock-hard and all I wanted was to be inside her, to fuck her.

She wrapped her arms around my neck and with her body flush against mine, I just didn't fight it anymore.

Picking her up, I carried her to the desk, throwing off everything that was in our way. I dropped her down on the edge as she tugged my shirt over my head.

I flicked open the catch of her jeans and yanked them down her thighs until they were all the way off. She moaned my name as I pressed my palm to her wet core. The panties she wore were soaked. Sliding a finger beneath the fabric, I traced over her clit, hearing her gasp as I went down to enter her. I pushed a single finger inside her, followed by a second, then a third, stretching her to take my dick. She thrust against my hand as if she couldn't get enough of me, and I knew I couldn't get enough of her.

"Please!"

I loved hearing her beg and moan.

After pulling my fingers from her tight cunt, I stroked over her clit, staring into her eyes, watching her as she let go. She didn't come straight away and I worked her pussy until I knew she was close. I didn't tear my gaze away, drinking in every single part of her until she finally came apart, and it was such a breathtaking sight.

So beautiful.

Once I opened my pants, I pulled my cock out, and in one thrust, I was balls deep within her tight walls and we were both moaning.

The angle wasn't right, so I moved us, pulling out of her, flipping her over so she was bent over the desk. After spreading the cheeks of her ass, I admired her pussy and asshole. Sliding back into her cunt, I groaned. We both did, and it was perfect. Holding on to her hips, I pounded inside her, going as deep as I could and fucking her harder than before.

When I felt I was close to coming, I slowed down. Slicking up my fingers, I pressed them across her asshole, and she cried out. I pushed a finger against her tight ring of muscles, and she fought me at first. With my other hand, I reached between her thighs and found her clit, stroking over her as I teased her ass.

I felt her answering pulse as her pussy tightened around my cock.

"You know I'm going to fuck this ass one day, Emily. It's going to be owned by all of us, just as you already are. We own you. You belong to all of us, and we're not going to let you get away." With that, I strummed her clit and pushed a finger in and out of her ass as I pumped inside her.

I was so close, and when she came, screaming my name, I followed her over the edge, relishing every single pulse and wave.

Emily had owned my heart and now, I was more than sure she'd taken possession of my soul.

Chapter Six

Emily

I ate breakfast on my own. River was there, but he didn't eat. The rest of the day, we hung out. It was hard for me to be mad at him for so long. He kept me entertained even though inside I was freaking out.

Caleb, Gael, and Vadik had all disappeared. I didn't know where they'd gone.

As I changed for dinner, alone, I recalled River's warning.

"You're going to have to learn to keep hold of your shit in front of our men. If you don't, it won't take long for our enemies to discover we have a weakness."

He wanted me to treat them like kings. In this world, they were. They wouldn't hurt me, but their enemies would make sure I suffered. It didn't take a genius to work out the drill.

Running fingers through my hair, I settled on a black dress. It had a low neckline and a slit up the side.

I didn't know why I want to get under their skin. They'd come and got me at the first opportunity, and that meant they hadn't discarded me like I meant nothing. All the pain of the last seven years, it felt like it was for nothing.

Ashley.

I didn't want my happiness to come at a cost for her. I wasn't a selfish person, or at least, I tried not to be. Ashley deserved to have a man who would love her, who would be completely devoted to her. Not a man who'd take her virginity and discard her.

With my hands clenched into fists, I turned toward the door as it opened. Vadik was my new babysitter. He took in my hands.

"You're already angry with me?"

"Not at you." I opened my hands, hating how easy it was for me to get angry. I hadn't felt this way in a long time.

"Ashley?"

I nodded.

"We're going to get her back."

This made me laugh.

"Don't, Emily."

"I can't help it. You don't know where he's taken her, and you're telling me we're going to get her back. Do you have any idea how stupid it sounds?" I asked.

Vadik sighed. "He wants something from her."

"He could rape her to get it." I shook my head. "I don't want to talk about this now." My stomach chose that moment to start moaning in protest. I wasn't going to stop eating.

"I know you're angry with us, but we will fix this."

"You shouldn't have bargained with her life."

This time, Vadik laughed. "Look, you can be angry with us. We can all take it. You think we haven't taken worse in the time you've been away?"

I stared at him, my gaze wandering down his body, wondering if he had more scars than River or the same kind.

"But don't for a second believe we're the good guys. We had to give you up, but none of us wanted to. After seven years, someone offered us a chance and we took it."

I couldn't help but laugh again. "Yeah, you took it without truly understanding the consequences of what you've done."

He stepped up toward me. He gripped my neck and now he was kissing me. I couldn't deny I relished their dominance. It sent a thrill down my spine. I liked them taking charge, taking me.

I thought about River and Gael, now Vadik. None of them had wanted to know about the seven years between us. They just wanted me, craved me, and that was a heady experience. It almost made me not hate them. I did. I hated and loved them, and that was a bad combination to have.

Like now, I wanted to do a lot of bad things with Vadik, but at the last second, just as I was giving in to my needs, he pulled away, creating a distance.

"It's time for you to have dinner."

Without waiting for me to respond, he took my hand and led me down the hallway, toward the dining room.

I caught sight of the soldiers. There were a lot more of them than there had been this morning.

As we got to the dining room, I paused. It was only me and my men. No one else. Dinner was spread on the table and at the click of Caleb's fingers, he forced everyone else to leave so it was just us.

The door closed and the sound echoed in the quiet room.

Caleb stood, arms resting behind him. He had an air of authority. Even though we were all the same age, he seemed older, scarier, more dangerous. I didn't know what had changed from yesterday to now, but seeing him standing in his castle, he looked totally different. The suit as well, it took me by surprise.

His gaze ran up and down my body. I may as well have been naked.

"You look beautiful."

With hands clenched into fists, I wasn't going to succumb to his compliments.

"Where's Ashley?" I asked.

He smiled. "Eat."

"No."

"Don't make this any harder than it has to be."

"No one is watching us. I don't have to show you respect. River gave me the drill of how it's supposed to be." I folded my arms. "Now tell me where my friend is."

He put his hands together. I noticed the large fingers and couldn't help but wonder how many people he'd killed with those very hands. I shouldn't have even cared and yet, here I was, wondering. They had all struck a deal with the devil to get me here. Ashley's life was at stake.

"You know, we're the ones who saved her. You could have been on your own all this time."

"Cut the crap, Caleb. Where is she?"

His smile forced me to take a step back, but then I straightened my spine. I wasn't afraid of any of these men. I wouldn't back down.

The instant he took a step toward me, all I wanted to do was run and cover. I stayed perfectly still, even as he invaded my space. Neither of us was the same people. We were different.

I waited.

He reached out and took a stray curl, brushing it behind my ear. "We'll find Ashley."

"That actually means you don't have a fucking clue where she is."

He licked his lips and I hated myself for watching, for wanting him.

I didn't fight him as he gripped my waist, the first touch startling me.

"Leave us," he said.

I glanced around the room to watch Vadik, Gael, and River each respond to his request.

The instant the echo of the door sounded, I was pressed up against a wall his rock-hard cock against my stomach. I was shocked by just how hard he was.

I wasn't expecting it.

"I'm not going to fuck you. Not with what you did to Ashley."

I thought he'd be angry, but instead, he merely laughed.

"That's okay with me. I can wait." His face was pressed against my neck, and I gasped as his tongue traced over my pulse. "Do you have any idea how long I've fucking waited to just hold you?"

Only, he didn't just hold me. His hands traced down my body, going to my hips, squeezing them tightly before reaching the hem of my skirt and slowly lifting it up. It was on the tip of my tongue to tell him no, but I didn't. I couldn't believe I didn't stop him even as he sank down to his knees, so he was right in front of my pussy.

I was wearing panties, and with ease, he tugged them right out of his way.

"I can handle you hating me right now, Emily. I expect it. You're right. We did use your best friend for our own needs, and I'm not going to apologize for that. Especially when I don't want to." He groaned. "Look at this sweet pussy. It's made to be fucked."

I couldn't help but cry out as he spread my legs and his hand touched me right between the thighs. He didn't linger. Instead, he spread the lips wide as he moved up, lapping at my pussy. His tongue tracing across my clit. At first, I clenched my hands into fists but then I had no choice but to sink my fingers into his hair as he moved his mouth over me.

"No, this isn't any good."

He pulled away from my touch, and within a

matter of seconds, I was spread out on the dining room table like some festive offering. The top of my dress was pulled down, revealing my tits, which he cupped before sucking each bud into his mouth. His tongue traced across each mounded tip before biting down. Each touch set me on fire.

All I wanted to do was tell him to fuck me, but I held the words which were locked in my throat.

Caleb moved down my body and now that I was lying down, he could maneuver me into any position he liked. He gripped my ass, squeezing it tightly as his face pressed against my core and lapped up at my pussy.

"You have no idea how many times I thought about this moment. About getting you right here, where I want you."

"Please."

"I'm going to give it to you, baby. I promise." His teeth caused a slight jolt of pain but rather than turn me off, it did the opposite. I couldn't believe I'd already had sex today, but as Caleb pushed me toward another orgasm, I didn't care how weak I was. It felt incredible. The way he touched me. The instant hit of attraction and need.

I craved every single second of it.

He didn't stop. When I did finally come, I was shocked by such raw emotion that before I could control myself, I burst into tears.

I expected him to run off. To tell me to get over it, but instead, I was wrapped up in his arms as we sat on a chair.

"I know I've fucked up with you, Emily, and I'm sorry. I will find Ashley again. Dead or alive."

I tensed up.

He helped me to my feet, cupped my face, tilted my head back, and brushed his lips across mine.

I didn't tell him to stop. I watched him leave and quickly rearranged my dress so I looked somewhat decent.

It wasn't long before Vadik, Gael, and River returned, but I'd lost my appetite. Without another word to them, I left the dining room, going straight to my room. I closed the door, pressing my fist against the hard wood.

Seconds passed.

Maybe even minutes before I finally stripped out of my clothes and climbed into bed.

Pulling up the covers, I heard a clock ticking. I didn't know if it was in my head or actually a clock in the room. Either way, it was mocking me. Ashley was in danger and I was lying in a beautiful bed, surrounded by the men who claimed to love me, while she was with a man only interested in her virginity. I was angry.

I was enraged by the world and all the men in it.

Even as I knew my anger had reached a new level, I couldn't help but also be grateful that I was here, and that was the biggest guilt I carried. I was happy to be here, I just wished it hadn't come at the price of my best friend.

****

Caleb

Our parents weren't dead, per se. They may have wished to be after the hell and continued hell we put them through.

I moved down the long corridor of the doctor's office in Crude Hill, typing in the code that only my friends, a few trusted minions, and I knew. The door gave the sound of admittance. It was dark, and I flicked on the light, making my way downstairs to find my father, sitting in his chair.

There didn't need to be any changes. Their medication kept them perfectly docile. Completely lucid, but unable to do anything with their murdering thoughts. It was genius. Gael had come up with the idea. He knew a scientist guy who was working on a new formula. It was similar to the date rape drug, but we'd decided to buy the man instead to start making different kinds of chemistry, not the kind that hurt women.

I always liked to wait until it was injecting time. When my father believed he had a chance of making it out of here alive. First, the drug would have to wear off completely. The design didn't allow for a slow awakening of the body. One moment, it was completely numb, the next, it was alive and ready to do battle, but the transition could also make a person sick. I'd seen it all done. My daddy was a little guinea pig. If I hadn't betrayed him and taken over his life and businesses, I believed he'd be proud of me. I'd finally found a way to keep my enemy from ever knowing a moment's peace or happiness, and in return, it made me immensely happy. He was the only one down here, at my request. The others were put in separate rooms, visited when one of us wanted to play.

I knew we were due for a visit. It had been a couple of days, and rather than take Emily against her wishes, I knew my father would be a good stress reliever. He'd take my mind off of actually wanting to have sex.

After grabbing the chair, I dragged it to where he sat, turned it, and straddled the seat, resting my arms across the back as I watched him.

He didn't even twitch, but I knew he watched me.

"I think it's time we had a talk." I got up, going toward the row of needles, all of them labeled. I grabbed the one that I knew worked, picked up his useless arm, and plunged it inside, spilling the right amount of medicine I needed to have a conversation with him, but not enough to wake up his body.

I wasn't afraid of my father. Far from it. I was the one who had helped to bring the daddies down here. Without me, we wouldn't have been able to take over. It had been a battle, one I wanted.

"Hello, old man," I said.

"I will fucking kill you."

I couldn't help but laugh. His threats weren't needed here. "Really?"

"One day, you're going to make a mistake. You'll forget and you can't keep me down here forever."

"I know. One day, I intend to kill you, but I'm waiting for when you can feel the most amount of pain and not live through it. That's all I'm waiting for. When that day comes, you'll be set free to go to hell."

"And you think I'll be going alone?"

"I know there's going to be a special seat in hell for me. I look forward to it." I cracked my knuckles as I watched him. "She's back."

He didn't have any reaction. Even after all this time, my father was still sound of mind. No reaction, but I knew he was thinking, plotting, planning.

"It can't be going according to plan."

"Why is that?"

"You're here and not fucking your woman, or do you let your friends take care of the manly parts?"

I didn't react even though I wanted to.

He chuckled. "Rather than be balls deep inside your woman's pussy, you've come to see your old man. It makes one wonder what you fucked up on."

I stayed quiet. I knew better. He was trying to provoke me so I'd make a mistake.

Not going to happen. I had this shit covered.

I wouldn't mess this up.

"You know, when we had our woman, you were lucky we got any work done. We couldn't get enough of her. She belonged to us." He let out a sigh. "I wonder what she'd think of you doing this to me."

"Lucky for me, I don't have to worry about my mom coming back. I wonder what she'd have to say about you."

"She loved me," he said.

"Yeah, but what would she think of you taking away her son's love. Huh? The threat you had to Emily."

"You think that threat is gone?" He laughed. It was a forced sound. "You think all those soldiers show you love and respect? You still have a lot to learn. All of you do, but like always, you thought you knew best, when the truth is none of you know shit."

"You think we don't know that you've got men all around? We'll find them all."

"No, you won't. The thing about loyalty is it's spread a little too thin all around. People have a tendency to jump when the ship appears to be wobbling. One of you will fuck up, and it's going to cost Emily her life."

"Whatever deal you made to take her out of the picture isn't going to happen. We've already got it covered."

This made my father laugh. I didn't like the sound.

"You're a stupid, lovesick puppy. There's only one person I know who would even deem to make a deal with you." He stared at me, almost as if he could see right through me, and knew every single part. "Earl."

I didn't like this, but rather than protest, I kept silent.

"Yeah, he'd be the son of a bitch to make any kind of deal with you." He coughed. I made a note to arrange for some more fluids. I didn't want him to die on me all of a sudden, not when I had plans. "You're a fucking stupid boy. The only thing that man ever wanted was a little virgin to play with. Seeing as you're here and not fucking your cunt, I'd say he took someone of hers and now she's pissed." He laughed. "Well, I guess it had to happen. You had to fuck something else up that you're not prepared for."

I got up and went back to the injections, finding the one I needed.

I grabbed his arm, which was useless.

"Go ahead, keep injecting me, but you better warn that scientist of yours that it will only be so long before this shit starts to have no effect. You'll either kill me, or you're going to die at my hands, Caleb."

I plunged in the needle and he was back to being nothing more than a living corpse.

"You're wrong, Daddy. I know what I'm doing."

I left him in his chair. He could wait a little longer to be moved to a bed to sleep and to have any comfort.

He pissed me off and when he did that, he knew there was always a punishment.

Chapter Seven

Emily

Rolling over, I opened my eyes. I hadn't closed my curtains last night and sunlight streamed through my bedroom window.

Caleb.

One by one, my men came to my thoughts, until I finally thought of Ashley.

After throwing the covers off, I went to the bathroom, took care of business, washed my hands, brushed my teeth, and came back to the closet.

I settled on sweats, leaving my bedroom and heading down the long corridor. I passed men patrolling the grounds and I ignored them.

I'd gotten used to there being no guns in England. I didn't like how unsettled I felt. I needed protection.

Entering the dining room, I saw Gael, Vadik, and River seated, also Caleb.

They had all come to my bedroom last night, knocking on my door, calling out my name. I hadn't responded to any of them.

I didn't acknowledge them now. I took a seat and reached for a bowl of fruit. Seconds later, Gael put a cup of coffee beside me.

I thanked him and started to eat the fruit as they continued to enjoy their full breakfast.

I wasn't hungry.

"Today, I want you to check the ports. All of them. Any register, and then go for the bribes," Caleb said.

I turned toward him to see him looking at Gael.

"You do the city. I want to know where he took his last steps." This order was given to River.

Vadik had street detail.

"I'm going to reach out to our contacts from here."

They all nodded, stood, and I watched them leave, one by one.

"You're going to find her?" I asked.

"I promised you we would. We had a deal, and I don't like that he betrayed us. I'll find Earl and Ashley." Caleb wiped his mouth with a napkin.

"Where are you going?"

"To do some work. I can't sit around here all day doing nothing."

"What about me?" I asked. This wasn't exactly how a kidnapping went.

"Enjoy the grounds. For your own safety, don't go too far. Explore. Our home is your home, just be careful."

He reached into his pocket and I didn't know what I expected him to give me, but it certainly wasn't a knife. "For your protection."

I took it, about to thank him, but he was already gone.

Piercing a piece of fruit, I took a bite, not tasting it.

Why give me a knife? Was it not safe for me to return? I didn't like not having all the answers, and right now, I felt like I was in the dark. Rather than finish my breakfast, I got up, taking my coffee and leaving the dining room.

I would've helped clear the table, but past experience taught me that people had jobs to do. I remembered helping and my father catching me once back home. Rather than punish me, I had to watch as he whipped the young girl who'd been working for us. She hadn't been able to sit down for a couple of weeks because of the beating. The guilt had consumed me whenever I looked at her. One day, she did disappear. I only hoped that she'd found some peace. I suspected my father killed her, but I liked to live on the edge of disillusion. It was a nice place.

Stepping out of the dining room, I paused as I looked at the soldier at the door, complete with a gun. A knife couldn't compete with his weapon, besides, I didn't want to kill anyone.

Rather than bug Caleb, which was what I wanted to do—I wanted to piss him off and annoy him, but instead, I found myself wandering the walls of his family home. It was a big, lavish house, complete with so much art and fancy shit. It wasn't a house, but a museum of dick measuring.

I discovered a library, another large dining room, complete with a bigger table, which I assumed was for entertaining. A games room, several other rooms, and I entered the back, coming to a stop when I saw it was a large greenhouse. The moment I stepped inside, the warmth consumed me, and the smells of the plants and the earth were heady.

Keeping a hold of my knife, I stepped through the foliage, seeing plants labeled. I reached out and I touched a single rose on a bush. It was a bright red, almost like the color of blood. Stroking the petal, I took a quick step back when I heard a noise.

Like a scuffling sound. My heart raced as I felt it coming in close.

Sliding the blade open, I went in for the attack as arms wrapped around my waist. I was suddenly lifted in the air and slammed to the ground. I didn't allow myself time to think, I attacked. Pressing the blade to an arm, I heard a sudden hiss. I tried to get to my feet, only to be pushed to the ground again. This time, whoever it was that had me trapped straddled me. I wriggled and the blade was knocked out of my hands.

My arms were pushed out, and I was spread out before whoever this was, only to come to a stop when I finally caught the face of my attacker.

I was panting.

"Drake?"

"Emily?"

He was distracted enough that I knocked him off me and got to my feet. I grabbed my knife and stared at him.

This was the hothead from high school. The love child with an attitude problem. Only as I stared at him now, he didn't look like a giant mess or a statistic waiting to happen.

He was cleanly shaven. Dressed in a suit. Composed.

"Well, well, well, I heard the rumor you were back, but I didn't believe it."

"What are you doing here?"

He clapped his hands. "That's right. You've been gone. You don't know the latest. I work here."

"You're a gardener?"

He burst out laughing.

"He works for us," Caleb said, drawing my attention behind me.

"I'm sorry about putting my hands on your woman," Drake said. "I saw someone trespassing and I know how protective you are of this place. I was just doing my job."

"Thank you. You may leave."

"You're looking good, Emily. Damn, if only I'd gotten my hands on you in high school."

"I would have slit your throat," I said.

"That just turns me on." He winked as he left.

I couldn't quite believe what I'd just seen.

I turned toward Caleb.

"Drake. Seriously? You hired him?"

"He's loyal."

"He's a piece of shit."

"People change."

"You do remember the same guy in high school, right? The one with the serious problems?"

Caleb chuckled. "We have been able to channel his issues into something more enjoyable."

I shuddered. "I can't believe he touched me."

"He touched you? Where?" The humor had gone from Caleb's eyes.

"I don't mean like that. He … we fought, okay. I just, I never liked Drake. Never could trust him. He was always after making a name for himself."

"He has made a name for himself. He's turned into a trusted ally."

I couldn't stop shaking my head. It was wrong. "I can't believe this." I turned to look around at the greenhouse. "You created this?"

"Yes."

"You?"

"I had help and guidance from a gardener, but I maintain all the plants and flowers here."

"Why?"

"It makes me happy."

"Right, and anything that makes you happy deserves your time."

"You're pissed again."

"I'm trying to understand."

"None of us wanted to let you go, Emily. None of us. We didn't have a choice."

I spun back around to face him. "Where are your parents?"

"I don't want to get into that right now."

"You're really going to have to." I folded my arms, but he merely took a step back.

"There are things you're not ready to know."

He left and I was alone in his garden, none the wiser as to what he meant.

****

Gael

My knuckles were bruised, but I had information. Caleb wasn't going to like it. Washing off the blood, I looked up and saw the colors erupting over my face from the beating I'd taken. I'd won in the end, but there was nothing wrong with letting my opponent believe he was winning. It wasn't fair, I'd admit, but it was fun.

He thought he could actually beat a Monster and win. It was laughable. He was now resting on the bottom of the ocean floor, unless a nice big shark was eating him. I liked to think something was getting use out of the pointless waste.

At the creak of the door, I grabbed my gun and aimed. No one came into my bedroom, least of all my bathroom. I paused.

Emily was staring right at me. Her hands were raised and I saw a slight tremble in them. I instantly hated myself for threatening her. "I'm sorry."

"It's okay."

"No, it's not. I'm not used to people coming into my bathroom."

"I take it you're a private person."

I shrugged. "Not really. I just don't have women in my room."

She folded her arms. "Are you okay?"

"I see you don't want to talk about the no-women comment."

"You can tell me all you want that you weren't with anyone. I know it's been years and you've got certain needs. I don't need to be lied to."

"Not lying to you. No one would even begin to compare to you. You're all I've ever wanted."

"Cut the crap, Gael. Why is Drake working for you?"

I laughed. I couldn't help it. "You've met him again. You got a little crush?"

"He's an asshole."

"You'd be surprised what he can find out." I dried my hands on the towel and turned toward her.

Her gaze went all over my face. "What happened?"

I opened my mouth and closed it.

"It's Ashley, isn't it?"

"I've got to go and see Caleb."

I tried to go past her but she put a hand on my chest. "Don't, please. Tell me."

I tossed the towel across the room. This information was for Caleb, but I didn't want to hurt her any more than I already had. I knew using her friend wouldn't exactly win us any respect in her books, but we'd done it anyway, and we'd fucked up.

"He had a boat waiting for him at the docks. Paid someone nearly ten grand to keep it quiet. I was able to get the information about the boat, who paid him, and where they dropped him off."

"What? So, Earl Valentine is out on open water?"

"Yes."

"Ashley hates the water. It scares her."

"We're going to get her back."

She hit me in the chest. Once, then twice, before stepping back. Her scream cut me to the core. She spun on her heel, but I couldn't let her go like this. I knew we were the ones who caused her pain. I grabbed her hand, pulling her back against me, and I took possession of her lips.

"No!" She pulled away.

Her lips already looked swollen.

She stared at me, and I expected her to slap me again, but instead, she moved closer, wrapping her arms around my neck and kissing me back as if her life depended on it.

I held her tight against me, lifting her up, sinking my fingers into her hair, breathing her in.

She wrapped her legs around me, and I walked her back, going into my bedroom. I sat down on the bed, kissing her, sliding my tongue across her lips. She opened up for me, and I moaned.

Emily rubbed her pussy against my dick. One of her hands released my neck and glided down, going to my cock.

"Fuck!"

"I was going to ask for an update, but I see that you're busy," Caleb said.

Emily broke the kiss to look behind her.

Caleb closed the door, but he didn't leave. Instead, he went to sit down on a chair.

"I was coming to you," I said.

"But you had Emily, and I have to say, whatever you've got to tell me can wait." He pointed at us. "Continue."

Emily climbed off my lap. I expected her to leave, but she was full of surprises as she started to remove her clothes. She was wearing an ugly-ass shirt and the largest pants I'd ever seen. She wriggled out of them.

Her glare was on Caleb, but it didn't stop her.

She turned back to me and I saw the anger on her

face. I wanted to take it away.

"If he wants a show, then we'll give him one," I said.

She stared at me, then back at Caleb. At first, I thought she was game for this, but I now saw I was so wrong about her.

In the next second, she shook her head, reaching for her clothes. "I'm not a whore. I don't perform."

"You're not going anywhere," Caleb said.

I wanted to tell him to fuck off, but she threw her sweater at him. "You don't get to tell me what to do."

"No?" He stood up. "Let's get one thing straight here, Emily. You are ours. You belong to us. You always have. You're not leaving this room. You either fuck him or you fuck me. Which one is it going to be?"

I'd never seen Caleb like this. Sure, he had a temper, but most of the time, he was able to keep it in check. This wasn't him in control. This was him on the verge of doing something fucking stupid and I'd hate to lose him to something stupid.

I saw her deep inhalations as she glared at him. I had to wonder which one she'd pick. I expected her to go to Caleb, but then she came back into my arms.

Her mouth attacked mine and rather than fight her, I ran my hands up her back, feeling her against me.

She was only doing this to spite Caleb, but I didn't care. Not as she ground on my dick. I was hard, and all I wanted to do was fuck her. To completely consume every single part of her. She was so beautiful.

Emily let go of my face and attacked my clothes. She got my pants open, her fingers wrapped around my length as she ground down.

I wasn't about to be outdone, and I cupped her between the thighs, wanting to touch every single part of her and not let a part of her go. She was so fucking precious.

Feeling how wet she was surprised me. She hated Caleb, but that didn't mean he didn't turn her on. She was on fire.

Breaking from the kiss, I held her still as I looked over her shoulder to find Caleb, cock in hand, watching us. The angle he sat in would mean he'd see everything. I plunged two fingers inside her, relishing her cries of pleasure.

It wasn't enough. Just as I was about to make my move, Emily was there, beating me to it. She pushed my hands out of the way, held my cock into position, and took me balls deep inside her cunt.

She was tight, wet, and everything I wanted. Returning my hands to her hips, I guided her over my length, making her take all of me. Her nails sank into my shoulder as I used her pussy, fucking her harder than before.

I was so close to coming, but I was determined not to find release until she had. She growled my name and I took it. Keeping my cock inside her, I stilled any movements and started to tease her clit. My name spilled from her lips and it was the perfect sound. So right. So sweet. I could live my life like this. With her in my arms, my bed, taking me night after night.

The time we'd been apart hadn't eased the fire I felt for her. If anything, it made me more desperate for her.

I needed her more than anything else in the world.

Kissing her neck, I flicked over her pulse, feeling her orgasm starting to build. I watched her come all over my length. I loved the way she tightened around me. She was my everything. I loved her more than anything else in the world, and I'd do anything to make her happy.

Even as she used me to punish Caleb, I didn't care. I knew deep down that she loved us all. This pain would pass. We'd get Ashley back, Emily would belong to us, and we'd finally be free to be happy.

That was all I wanted.

With the path so clear, I gave in to my needs, and I came, feeling Emily shake above me as I held her in place. We hadn't used a condom and to my knowledge, none of us had. She was no doubt going to be pregnant soon. It was only a matter of time. I was happy, but part of me was afraid. My mother had died in childbirth. I didn't know if I could stand for Emily to die. She was everything to us. I hadn't told any of the guys because I knew they'd worry as well. I wanted their head in the game.

Chapter Eight

Vadik

For Caleb to be drinking scotch straight from the bottle, I knew something had to have gone down. Gael had given me the call to return home as he had the details we needed. The streets hadn't exactly been forthcoming with information. Everyone I spoke to gave me all the details I needed to know, but the information was useless and everyone knew that.

Earl Valentine didn't vanish off the face of the earth.

I knew he'd betray us. Could almost taste it the moment he offered us that deal, but we'd all been too desperate to even care.

Betrayal or not, we'd gone after the one person we loved more than anything.

Now, Emily was nowhere to be seen, Caleb drank, and Gael, well, he looked like the cat that got the cream and ran over at the same time. I didn't know what was worse.

"What's going on?" I asked. I usually didn't mind the silence, but since Emily's return, it had been hard to come by.

"Nothing," Caleb said.

"She will forgive you," Gael said.

"Shut up, Gael," Caleb said.

I looked between the two.

"This isn't nothing," River said.

"I don't need to discuss every single detail of our lives." Caleb glared at us before throwing back more alcohol.

"No, you don't normally have to, but you're drinking straight from the bottle." I pointed out the obvious.

"It's Emily," Gael said. "Caleb watched her have sex with me and immediately after, she ran out of the room. I haven't seen her."

I looked toward Caleb.

"You're being a dick to her, why?" Gael asked.

"She hates my guts right now."

"You're not the only one who made the decision and yet she's targeting you. Why?" Gael asked.

Caleb laughed and got to his feet. "Why do you think? I'm the easy target. I'm the one who makes the final decisions. I'm the one who fucking agreed with that piece of shit that Ashley would go with him. It's all on me."

"Let's stay on track," River said. "You had something."

I focused on Gael. I didn't like how weak we were looking or sounding. We had our disagreements. What family didn't? But getting Emily back wasn't supposed to tear us apart.

"He's got her out on one of his ships. The *Valentine*. He made sure we were busy with Emily. He took off. Our men were given the slip. He had some body doubles go to the home we agreed upon. While we were distracted, as were our men, he took Ashley out of the port, and he's now sailing somewhere. I've already called in a few favors. We're going to get a location within hours."

Caleb launched the bottle across the room. "I'm going to kill him."

"We can't do anything that will risk her life. We know that. He knows that." I tried to reason with him.

"He knows jack shit," Caleb said. He ran a hand down his face. Suddenly, he started to laugh. "Do you realize how stupid we sound? We jumped on the first man to offer us a chance to get our woman. It makes us look weak."

"When it comes to Emily, we are weak," River said.

"We don't even know if the threat is truly gone." Caleb growled. "When I find him, he better hope he's killed himself because I'm going to make him pray for death long before I grant it."

"We can't do anything rash," I said.

"Have you found her?"

We all turned toward the door at the sound of Emily's voice. She stood in the doorway. I'd been too distracted to hear her come in. She was messing with all of our heads, but if we weren't careful, we were all going to get killed and it wouldn't be her fault, but ours. She hadn't come back to us. We'd gone to her.

"We know where he's taken her," Caleb said.

She nodded. "Good. What's the plan?"

"You're not part of it."

"I want my cell phone," she said. "I want to know if I can at least get in touch with her."

"We don't have it," Caleb said. "We trashed all of your possessions."

"You're infuriating." She ran a hand down her face, clearly struggling to stay in control. She held her hands out. "I don't want to fight anymore. I … can we just all agree to work together to get Ashley back?"

"You want to be friends?" River asked.

"Yes."

"Friends that fuck?" Gael asked.

She winced.

Caleb snorted. "So, you've fucked my three best friends but are leaving me out."

"I don't want to argue with you," she said. "I don't want to fight."

"And you think I do?"

"How did you expect this to go, Caleb? You got me at the price of my friend. You had to know I wouldn't accept that."

"I did what I had to."

"At what price?" She sighed. "Do you even know if he kept to his end of the bargain? I can't leave the house, can I? I don't know the full extent of your fathers' powers, but I'm not safe here."

"You are safe."

I didn't like where she was going with this. It was a fear that we all had, but I didn't like her voicing it.

"I can't hide in here forever, Caleb. Neither can all of you. You've got a town to destroy." She took a step out of the room and I watched her go, wanting to help her, to offer her comfort, but there was nothing I could say. She was right, like always. We were fucked.

Caleb stared at the door. In the brief second he stared at her retreating back, I knew he was in pain. He hated being a disappointment to Emily, but that was what we all were. With Ashley gone, we had all fucked up, and we had to pay the price.

"I'm going to reach out to some of my boys," I said. "See if I can find out about any movement or agreement of a kill on a female."

I couldn't stand to be in the room anymore and I left, not looking back. There was only so much pain we could all stand, and I had to make it right, once and for all.

****

River

I found Emily in the music room. She sat at the piano, her fingers touching each key, letting the sound linger in the air before moving onto the next one. She stared across the room at me.

"Do I have to go to my room for being naughty? I didn't see any soldiers."

"No, I'm not here to tell you where to go. You can sit and enjoy."

She sighed and both of her hands landed on the keyboard.

As the last notes lingered out, sadness swept over me. She was so miserable. The tears in her eyes caught me off guard. I went to her, sitting beside her and wrapping my arm around her.

"Don't cry. Please, don't cry."

"I'm sorry."

"No, don't be sorry. You can cry. I just, I hate to see you so upset, especially when I know we're the cause."

She sniffled. "I promised myself I wouldn't cry, but I fucked up big time."

"None of this is on you."

"No? If I had pushed Ashley away, none of this would have happened."

"You're right, she'd have been dead. We wouldn't have thought to save her." I gripped her arm tightly.

"Don't say stuff like that."

"Why not? It's the truth. She'd have suffered along with her mother. You know the facts. We all do." I couldn't let her believe any other way would have been a happier option for Ashley. It wouldn't. "What you can't do is blame yourself for all of this. None of this is your fault. Life happens. Shit happens. Don't blame yourself."

She sniffled and wiped at her eyes. "I'm sorry."

"Don't be sorry either." I pushed some of her hair back off her shoulder.

"I'm not like this. Sad and miserable, yeah, that

has been me."

"You're normally sad and miserable?"

"Yeah, having four men give you up can cause a great deal of heartache." She sighed. "I always promised myself that if I got to see you again, I'd be different. I wouldn't let a single moment go by without telling you how I felt."

I tensed up. "How do you feel?" She looked up at me and I cupped her face, wiping away the tears. "No more tears."

"You know how I feel, River."

"I've got an idea, but I don't know completely."

She chuckled. "You just want me to say it, don't you?"

I winked at her. "It would be nice to know what my girl thinks of me."

She sighed. "You're a pain in the ass."

"I'm lovable."

Her gaze ran over my body. "Where's your knife?"

"I can cope without one being in my hands." I slid my fingers into my back pocket and held it up for her. Opening the blade, I rested it on top of the piano. "I always keep one close at hand, though."

"I get that." She rested her head against my chest.

No words were spoken. I guessed I wasn't going to hear them tonight. I didn't mind. We were still on her shit list. I got it. We'd all fucked up. Still, I didn't like how badly Caleb was taking it. I don't think he felt guilty for using Ashley for his own personal means. I think what he was upset most about was getting caught. He couldn't stand the idea of Emily hating him.

"I love you," she said.

At first, I wasn't sure I heard her correctly, but there was no mistaking the words that fell from her lips.

"I love you too," I said.

She lifted her head. "You didn't have to tell me if you didn't feel it."

"I do. Letting you go was the hardest thing I ever had to do."

Her laughter filled the air as she rolled her eyes. "You're kidding, right?"

"I'm being serious. No joking around."

"You were kidnapped. The stories of what happened to you during high school were the stuff of legends."

I shrugged. "Either way, I knew I was either going to die or make it out alive. With you gone and no easy way of getting you back, that was the nightmare."

"I find that hard to believe."

"The love of my life was out there somewhere and I couldn't get to you. None of us could. I knew without a doubt I wouldn't be able to stand by and watch you fall for someone else. Just the thought of it makes me want to kill."

"I'm not with anyone else. I never found anyone. Ashley said I should go on dates, but I couldn't. It felt like I was cheating." She pushed some hair off her face and I watched her stifle a yawn. "Do you think she's okay?"

I didn't know if I should lie to her or not. Earl had a bad reputation, but when it came to women, it was always a murky image. No one knew for certain the kind of man he was.

"I believe he's taking really good care of your friend."

"Do you believe that?"

"Yes. Her virginity is precious to him. To a certain extent, he needs her innocence, so he's going to do everything he can to treasure it." I was talking out of my ass. I knew I was, but I had hope. Hope or plain stupidity, I wasn't sure yet.

She put her hand on mine. "Thank you. It means a lot. I'm going to go to bed." She leaned over and kissed me before pulling away.

Sitting at the piano, I watched her go, wishing I was with her. She needed her space. I needed my own kind of sleep as well.

I hadn't really slept in years. Running a hand across the piano keys, I wondered if we'd ever find happiness. If Ashley died, we were all fucked. I knew that. It was why Caleb was losing control.

Earl had fucked us over. We all knew it, and right now, we were trying to save face and to win over the love of our lives.

He wanted to be the head of our group, but now, I couldn't help but wonder if he wished he was somewhere else.

Chapter Nine

Emily

Another new day.

The house today was eerily quiet. I didn't see any soldiers. I didn't know if they'd been given orders to disappear when they saw me coming. Did that scare them? I didn't know why I cared.

Running fingers through my hair, I stepped into the library, going straight to the computer.

My cell phone held all my numbers. I couldn't remember Ashley's by heart. Another of my many failings as a friend. She would have been able to tell me my number, the one for the library, the store where I worked, and our Chinese place we loved to order takeout from when she didn't feel like cooking. It wasn't often she didn't feel like cooking. I missed her food.

The cook the guys had made delicious meals, no doubt about it, but I missed my best friend.

With my fingers above the keys, I didn't know where to start.

Going with her name, I typed it in and immediately changed it to our new identity name. My old paranoia getting the better of me. My hands shook a little when I thought of Ashley all alone. She wasn't like us. She'd only been part of our lives at Crude Hill High for a few months, not long enough to get used to it.

Dropping my face into my hands, I felt the tears once again coming to the surface. I'd admitted to River last night that I loved him. It felt good telling him the truth, but again, the guilt. With Ashley in danger, I couldn't be happy. I refused to be happy.

Scrolling through the names that popped up, I was sure I caught sight of her on a social media page and clicked on it. It was the wrong person. Next, I went to the website of the restaurant where she'd worked. Her picture was there, but no details of how to get in touch with her.

"Are you in love with a girl now as well? Four men aren't good enough for you?"

I jumped out of my chair to see Drake sitting on one of the tables, eating a candy bar. "How long have you been there?"

"Long enough to know you're stalking some chick. I seem to recognize her. Did we go to school with her?"

"This is none of your business." I stood in front of the computer screen.

"Please, I know it's that Ashley chick. I know the deets. You're not breaking any code."

"Do they share all of this information with you?" I asked.

"Yep." He put the last piece of chocolate into his mouth and moved toward me. I didn't back away as he closed the distance between us. "What you have to do is know the right search to make. What are you looking for?"

"I'm not telling you."

"Emily, I'm actually trying to help you here. I'm not trying to cause you any trouble. You want to know about your friend. I'm offering you that chance, but if you want to be a bitch about it, be my guest." He held his hands up in surrender and turned to walk away.

"I'm sorry," I said. I couldn't let him walk away. "I'm trying to remember Ashley's phone number."

"It's why they invented cell phones."

"Mine has been destroyed."

He chuckled. "Those pesky men of yours." He tutted. "How does that whole thing work, anyway?

You're going to have to move."

"What?"

"Out of the way so I can do my thing."

"Oh." I took a step to the side and he sat in my chair. His fingers worked over the keyboard.

"So, how does it go? Do they all share you at once? A gang bang?"

"I don't have to answer this."

"Yeah, you kind of do. I'm helping you, after all, and I'm keeping you safe."

"You're helping me, and I don't need you to keep me safe."

He snorted. "Please. You didn't even realize I was watching you." He winked at me. "Don't worry, I didn't see too much."

"Are you trying to insinuate that you've seen me naked?"

"Maybe."

"You're disgusting."

"Nothing of the sort, babe. Believe me."

"What happened to you? I can't believe they'd trust you with any of this."

"People change, Em. People grow up. It might also have to do with the fact that I killed my father." He clicked the *enter* button. "Nothing like being told how useless you are every single day. He told me I was a waster, so I decided to show him exactly what a waster I was. It was cathartic."

"Great, you start to feel better by killing your dad, and because of mine, I was sent to another country. You've got to love the parents, don't you?"

"That sounds a lot like sarcasm."

"It is." I put my hands on my waist, wanting this conversation to be over.

He shoved away from the desk. "There you go.

Her number, but I'd hurry up."

"Do you have a cell phone?"

He handed me a cell phone, and I quickly dialed the number, not caring where he got it or what it was going to cost me.

I put the cell phone to my ear and it rang, and rang, and rang. When I thought it was about to go to voicemail, someone picked up.

"Ashley. Ashley. Please, tell me that it is you."

No one said a word.

I clenched my hand into a fist.

"Is this you, Valentine?" I asked.

He let out a chuckle. "I am surprised."

"You listen to me closely. Leave her alone."

"You're not the one to be making demands of me, little girl. I can do to Ashley whatever the hell I want."

"No. You will leave her the fuck alone, you piece of shit. She has nothing to do with this. Nothing."

"My cock is hard, and I think it's only fair that I go and taste a cherry."

"No—"

He hung up.

The line just went dead.

"No! No! No!" I went to throw the cell phone, but Drake caught it.

"I'm not going to have you do that. I take it Earl answered the phone."

"Are you working for him?" Dread filled my stomach. What if Drake was a traitor? Would he work both sides? I couldn't put it past him.

"No. Of course not."

"You could be lying."

"I swore my loyalty to your men." He pocketed his cell phone. "I may have been a dick in high school, but if anyone had given me the time of day, they'd have realized I'm the fucking shit when it comes to getting stuff done, and I never let down the team. I'm not double-tagging. Nothing in this life comes for free."

"What do you want?" I asked. I knew there would be a price for the phone and the number.

"Simple, fuck Caleb. Forgive Caleb. Get off your little pedestal and realize that man loves you. He wants to make it right with you, but as usual, you're being a cunt."

"Don't be an ass."

"Stop acting like you would've done something better."

"I would never have used my friend to get what I wanted."

"No? But you would've used me? I like to think I'm close to all four of them. Don't assume you would've done something different. You're not in their shoes. You're in your own. Keep your opinions to yourself. They're not warranted here." He patted my arm. "I expect Caleb to be of sound mind and a tired dick tomorrow. I'll be watching."

Drake left the room, but I had a feeling he hadn't gone far.

I didn't want to do what he demanded, but I also didn't want to owe him anything either.

This was my own fault, and now I had to deal with the consequences and it fucking sucked.

I left the library and went in search of Caleb. I expected him to be gone, but he sat in his office, looking over some paperwork. His head rested in his hand.

For a few seconds, I didn't make him aware of my presence. I watched him.

He looked up, seeing me there. He put the paperwork down.

"Emily."

I stepped into the office.

"Hey."

I hesitated in closing the door but finally pushed it closed. I didn't know where Drake went, but I certainly didn't trust the bastard.

He'd proven to be way too slippery.

Caleb stood, rounding the desk. "What can I do for you?"

I licked my lips. "I wanted to apologize for everything."

"You do?"

"Yes. I was angry. I still am. I … I'm sorry."

He folded his arms. "What is going on?"

"I called Ashley."

His brows went up.

"Drake, he er, he was able to find me her phone number. I used his cell phone, and yeah, Valentine was on the line."

Caleb turned away, grabbing his cell phone and pressing a button. "Get Drake in here now."

"What are you doing?"

"I want the number. I haven't been in contact with Earl Valentine. He should have come to me. I would have dealt with it."

"I'm trying to apologize."

"Emily, you don't have to do that."

"No, I do. Look, I know this is going to sound awful. Drake wants me to fuck you and he did it because he got me that number, but I'm not actually here about that."

"Wait a minute!"

"No, let me finish."

"Drake gave you an order to fuck me? He didn't do this willingly?"

I closed my hands together, trying to compose myself, but it was hard to do. Caleb was pissing me off, when I just wanted to apologize to him, to settle this once and for all.

"Will you stop?"

"No, no one tells you what to do."

"Apart from you and the others."

"It's different. You're ours." He grabbed the phone again and I was starting to lose my temper. This wasn't going how I wanted it to go.

He was already on the phone with someone else, barking out instructions. None of them made much sense to me.

Taking a step back, I headed toward the door, willing to call defeat, but I got to the exit and stopped. I wasn't a quitter, not really.

Closing the door again, I marched up to Caleb. As he talked, I grabbed the phone, throwing it away as I captured his face, drew him close, and kissed him. I thought he'd fight me, but he didn't. His hands went to my shoulders, one sinking into my hair, kissing me back.

I grabbed his shirt and tore it open. Buttons sprayed across the room in all different directions.

"Wait, Emily, you don't have to do this. I'll kick Drake's ass."

"No, you won't. We're doing this and then we're going to work together to figure out how to help my best friend. That's how this is going to work. Now you can either kiss me or I swear I will leave it another seven years before you ever see me naked, let alone fuck me."

Seconds passed after my threat.

Which one was he going to pick?

Me or dealing with Drake?

Which one meant more to him?

I waited.

He turned toward me, kissing me deeply, but I wasn't fooled. I knew he could be taming me, only the kiss didn't stop. This wasn't a rush, but a conquering.

His tongue traced across my lips and I opened up. No more fighting.

Drake was right. Caleb had done what anyone would do in his position. I would've sold my boys' friends in a heartbeat without a moment's thought, Drake especially. I couldn't hate them forever. I'd only just gotten them back and I wasn't going to lose them again.

****

Caleb

Drake's demise was at the top of my list. I was going to kill him. No doubt about it, but as I kissed Emily and she responded, I couldn't hate him. He'd given her back to me. Whatever he'd said to her, I was going to find out. When we were teenagers, Drake's transformation was huge. The moment he killed his father, it was like the man stepped in to take care of the young boy, and because of that, he'd been a very valuable asset.

He had a high number of kills under his belt and his ability to go to places undetected was why we'd put him in charge of Emily's security detail. At least until we knew the full threat she faced at the hands of our fathers.

I couldn't get enough of her kisses.

The office wasn't the place I wanted to take her, but I didn't want to move from this spot and risk someone ruining our little bubble.

After picking her up, I dropped her onto the edge of my desk, throwing everything out of the way as I cupped her face and kissed her once again.

This was going to be the first time of many.

Her nails sank into my flesh and I shoved the skirt she wore up her thighs. At least she wasn't wearing sweatpants any longer and had started to wear some of the clothes we'd purchased for her.

She moaned as the tips of my fingers touched across her clit. She spread her legs even wider.

The skirt wasn't tight and flowed around her legs. I pushed the fabric of her panties aside and touched her aching core.

When I'd watched Gael fuck her, I'd been out of my mind with jealousy and pleasure. I'd wanted to be with her, but if I could only watch until she forgave me, then that was what I was willing to do.

I knew I was willing to do whatever it took to win this woman. My feelings for her hadn't changed since high school. They'd gotten stronger, and now I had a brand-new determination not to lose her.

She was ours.

We'd do whatever it took to keep her.

I pulled the shirt free of her skirt and slid it over her head, throwing it across the room. It didn't matter where it landed.

The bra was in the way. I didn't care that it was lacy and looked sexy as fuck. I wanted her completely free and clear for me to play with.

I craved her.

With the bra gone, I pressed her tits together and flicked my tongue across each peaked nipple. They were rock-hard and she arched up, giving me better access to her body. I glided my tongue across one peak, then moved to the second before biting down on the hard bud.

She moaned my name. Her legs spread.

"Do you have any idea how many times I've thought about this? Wanted you here to fuck, to spread over my desk?"

"Please, Caleb."

"Do you want my cock?" I asked.

"Yes."

"Say my name."

"Caleb."

"That's right. It's me. I'm going to be the one fucking you, taking you." Sliding my tongue up her neck, I swirled over her pulse, sinking my teeth into her flesh. I wanted to leave my mark all over her, and that was all I could think about. She was everything to me, to us.

Letting her go, I kissed down her body, paying more attention to her tits, before I went down even further. She lifted up enough for me to slide the skirt right off her hips and throw it to the floor. If it weren't for the soldiers, I'd have her naked every single day.

With her legs spread, I stared at her pussy. Wet, swollen, and I was hungry for a taste of her. I opened her lips and took my first lick. Swiping my tongue through her folds, I tasted her, and she was even better than I imagined. As I nibbled on her clit, I used my teeth, creating just enough pain. Then I soothed it out by swirling around her nub before going down to her entrance and teasing her there.

I couldn't get enough.

Her pussy juices were all over my face and I lapped them up while my name was a constant mantra spilling from her lips.

Plunging two fingers deep in her cunt, I felt her pulse around me. The moment I made her come, I was going to use my cock, but not a moment too soon.

She wriggled on my fingers and I relished each pulse of her. Pushing my fingers in and out of her, I twisted them and stroked right where her G-spot was. Tantalizing her. This got her even wetter, and as I sucked on her clit, I knew she was close to coming. Rather than prolong her release, I took care of it, getting her off quickly.

I was also being selfish. As much as I wanted to

give her the best orgasm in the world, I also wanted to fuck her.

I knew I wasn't going to last and as she came, the pleasured sounds spilled from her lips, echoing around the room, and I didn't waste a second. I eased down my zipper, pulling my cock free from the tight confines of the clothes, and pressed the tip between her thighs. I plunged in and out of her before moving up to touch her clit with my tip. She was still in the throes of her orgasm. I was an expert at making a woman last, and I intended to make her as well, only, I couldn't wait any longer.

Gripping her hips, I slammed balls deep inside her, the tight heat of her cunt thrilling me, I held on to her hips in a death grip as I began to pound her. I wasn't slow at all. I took what I wanted.

Her pussy still was pulsing on my dick in little aftershocks of pleasure. I'd been waiting seven years for this. Seven long, exhausting, tiring years, and there was no way I could hold back. I fucked her hard and fast, but I couldn't control my need for her. Slamming to the hilt within her, I came, spilling every single drop of cum inside her, probably flooding her cunt with a lot of my spunk. I needed to start using protection. I didn't want her to die from a complicated pregnancy, like my mother did.

I pressed my face against her tits and groaned.

"Fuck," I said. "Next time will be a lot longer."

"Really?"

"Don't be a bitch." I lifted my head.

She chuckled. "I'm not being a bitch. Just wondering is all." Her hand lifted as if she was going to touch me. I wanted her to. Slowly, she placed her hand on my cheek and stroked. "Thank you."

"No, thank you." I kissed the inside of her palm. "I'm going to get her back, Em. I promise."

"I know."

"You can still be angry with me."

"No, I can't. Drake, even though he's an asshole, he's right. If this was the other way around, I would've done everything within my means to get you back. I know that. If it had been anyone else, I'd understand, but it's Ashley. She's a civilian, or as close to one as I can imagine."

I kissed her lips. "I'm going to get her back."

"But what if you can't? What if he's taken her far away and we can never find her?"

"Baby, don't underestimate who I am. I know how to get shit done and believe me when I say this, I'm going to get it done." There was no way I was going to let Emily down. Ashley had been a means to an end but if her safety was what my woman wanted, her safety was what she'd get.

Chapter Ten

River

I was going over Emily's security with Drake when Caleb came into the room, and without a single warning, clocked one of our best men right in the jaw. Drake would have seen it coming, but rather than defend himself, he took the punch. Interesting.

"Don't you ever fucking make a deal with Emily. Do you understand? Whatever you want, you get?"

Drake rubbed at his jaw. "You got what you wanted, didn't you?"

"Not because of you."

"Oh, please. That woman was on her high horse and she needed a fucking wake-up call. Guess what? I provided it. Damn. You sure know how to hit."

Caleb lifted his fist. I didn't make a single move to stop him.

"You made a deal with Emily?"

"It was an agreement, and in the long term, it helped your buddy out, but I guess he doesn't like having his dick sucked." Drake groaned. "I stated some facts to her. If she didn't like it, it's not my problem. Fuck." He tested out his jaw. It wasn't broken. "You going to kill me?"

"I should." Caleb looked ready to shoot him in the head.

"Then get on with it, or if you don't mind, I'm going to do my job and make sure she lives past you getting to Earl Valentine. Or do you want her brains splattered over the bedroom walls?"

"What are you talking about?"

I raised a brow at my best friend. "You finally got your time with Emily?"

"Are you slow?" Drake asked.

I looked at Drake. All throughout high school, I hadn't liked him. There were times I still didn't. He acted without thought half the time, and he had a lot of parental issues. Whenever we had parents to deal with and took Drake along, it always got messy. I accepted it, but that didn't mean I liked it.

One thing I couldn't deny, he was damn good at his job. Keeping Emily alive while we dealt with Valentine's betrayal was something we needed him for.

"In the past twenty-four hours, Drake's gotten word of three men entering our town. They've got the appearance of tourists, but Drake's not buying it. He's gone to check them out, and they're not tourists."

"How do you know?" Caleb asked.

"I know how tourists act, okay? This is my job, to keep Emily safe, and I'm telling you, she's at risk right now. Whatever deal you made with Valentine, either he did betray you, or your fathers have got some swing even from the inside. My suggestion is Earl helped you guys." Drake pointed at the file he'd given me. He always liked to create files for his work. Of course, he also enjoyed getting a nice big reward for a job well done. I couldn't fault him. His work was always flawless, for the most part at least.

"If Earl hadn't done his job, I believe we'd have already experienced multiple hits. Instead, we've got men traveling to our town. I think they are your fathers."

I didn't like this. If it was one of our fathers, it meant someone within our team, which was an extremely short list, was betraying us.

Caleb took the file from me and began to look over the report Drake had compiled. I'd give the fucker one compliment, he was always thorough and so far, he'd saved our asses multiple times. I often had to wonder why. Why did he want to save us when we'd hated his guts during high school? We still hated him at times, but still, I wouldn't get rid of him just because I couldn't stand him.

"I want Gael and Vadik," Caleb said. "They're going to deal with these men. Drake, you're on Emily watch, but this time, don't piss her off, and don't make any kind of deal with her. I can handle my own problems. River, you're with me."

"We going to our fathers, or having the short list of traitors coming here?"

"We're going there, and they're coming to us." Caleb slapped the file into Drake's hands. "Whatever she wants."

"And if she wants this body of mine?" Drake ran his fingers through his hair.

"You're begging for a beat down," I said, already walking away toward my car. I was itching to stab something, anything. I didn't like being betrayed. It left a bitter taste in my mouth, not to mention it also pissed me off in a big way.

We'd worked hard to get where we were.

Taking over from our fathers hadn't been easy. We had to be united against them, and that had taken time. We'd had to kiss their asses, all while plotting to bring them down. We'd put our lives at risk every single day until we finally changed the allegiance of the soldiers and minions, and overruled our fathers. Our mothers were all off enjoying spa days and travel. I'd even sent Amelia, my sister, out of town for the foreseeable future. This was no place for young girls. They were never to set foot in Crude Hill again. If they did, we'd kill them. We had given them an out that no one within our world had ever been granted. Of course, they didn't argue. Why would they?

We knew what we were doing.

After climbing behind the wheel, I started the engine as Caleb got into the passenger side. "You trust him?"

"We've got no other choice," he said, pulling on his seatbelt.

I didn't bother to put mine on.

Pulling out of the parking space, I pressed on the gas and sped right up to the gates. I clicked the button I had installed in my car, and they opened. I drove past them and waited long enough for them to close. I didn't like the thought of someone waiting for an opportunity to slip right past.

It had happened once.

A woman had gotten through the gates and been able to pass as a maid. She'd hidden in Vadik's bathroom and he'd gotten a nice scar as she'd stabbed him. The woman in question had been a soldier's mother. She'd been pissed about his death sentence, and well, since then, we'd been a little more cautious with our own safety.

Right now, my first priority was to make sure Emily didn't die. I wouldn't be able to handle her death and I couldn't even handle the thought of it. We needed to make sure she never got hurt in any way.

She meant everything to all of us. I didn't want to lose her. Not for a single second.

Tapping my fingers on the steering wheel, I drove in silence toward our destination. Our fathers' prison wasn't too far from our own home. We'd designed it purposefully so we could be close to them at all times.

Turning off the ignition, I climbed out and stared up at the house. On the outside, it looked like a beautiful, lavish estate. On the inside, death and decay clung to the walls.

I flicked my keys as I followed Caleb to the door leading to the basement. He keyed in the code, and I turned, looking around. Something caught my eye as the door opened, and I grabbed Caleb's arm.

"Wait."

"What for?"

"When did we install security leading into the bastards?" I pointed my finger at the camera. It rested between two exposed posts.

Caleb took a step toward it. It was a little too high but the angle was perfectly placed for the door.

Neither of us could reach it. Caleb looked around. Finding a plank of wood, he used it to poke the camera through and I caught it before it could smash.

It wasn't one of ours. I would've recognized it.

"Someone's been here," Caleb said. "Fuck. Is there any way of finding out how long that has been here?"

"Nope. We need to get this back to Gael or Vadik. They're the only ones of us who know their way around a computer."

"And Drake. He was able to get Ashley's phone number for Emily." Caleb looked toward the door.

I stared at the camera then at the door. "Wait, didn't you say you came here the other day?"

"I did."

"Did you see the camera?"

"River, I wasn't exactly looking."

Dropping the camera, I took off, heading toward the stairs, charging down them so fast I nearly fell, but I caught myself.

The light was on but I knew. I just knew our fathers weren't here.

"I guess we now know who is responsible for the three men mysteriously arriving," I said.

"Fuck." Caleb lashed out, kicking over a chair. I was as pissed as him, but I was able to control my rage.

"They're out," I said.

"I need the schedule. I need to know who was here last."

"Let's get out of here first." I had a sick feeling twisting my gut and I took off upstairs, clearing through the door. As I did, a blade was embedded into my shoulder as I was stabbed from behind. I growled out at the instant hit of pain, but I was used to feeling something like it.

Spinning around, I lashed out as Caleb came through the door. I turned and kicked it closed as Caleb took over, hitting our assailant. The man was big, strong, and knew how to fight.

I couldn't reach for the knife in my back. Instead, I grabbed the plank of wood and used it to slam across his head.

He turned toward me just as Caleb had gotten some rope. We all liked to carry certain tools. Mine was always a blade, while Caleb seemed to prefer rope. Caleb wrapped the thick knot around the man's throat.

I grabbed my knife from my back pocket and began to use it, slicing at him until finally, he didn't take another breath and slumped. We let him fall to the ground.

We were both panting.

My hands shook a little from the rush of adrenaline, but I brought up the schedule on my phone.

"Kyle," I said. "He's the one who was supposed to be here."

I struggled to get my breath, but as I turned to the kitchen, a smell I hadn't noticed before lingered.

Stepping inside, I walked toward the pantry and opened the door. Sure enough, there was Kyle, dead. His throat slit. A lifeless corpse.

"We need to get back to Emily," he said.

I couldn't agree more.

****

Gael

I was hurt. It stung like a son of a bitch, but I looked a lot more alive than my attacker. Going to the hotel rooms Drake had told us about, we'd discovered the men were indeed assassins. None I recognized, which meant they were old school, like our parents. I didn't like not knowing my attackers.

"You could always get Emily to come and stitch me up?" I asked as Vadik began sanitizing the needle. I loved my best friends, all of them, but I didn't want any of them coming at me with a needle, not today. I wanted to look all pretty for my woman.

Of course, the large gash on my right side would complain. The guy had nicked me with his blade as I'd strangled the life out of him. I'd taken that same blade and plunged it in his neck. I was pissed off that I'd been too distracted, and now look at me. I was a mess. I still wanted to be pretty for my woman.

"I'm not bringing Emily down here to see you like this. She'd freak out." Just as Vadik was getting ready to sew me up, complete with a nice large bottle of vodka for company, his cell phone rang. I took a nice big swallow of the liquid, but it was nasty stuff. I'd never been much of a vodka drinker myself.

"Fuck, you're sure?" Vadik stepped away from me. "You're okay." He looked at me and I raised a brow. "We've got a stab wound of our own. Get here soon."

He hung up his cell phone.

"Do I want to know?" I asked.

"I don't know what's going to annoy you more.

This"—he plunged the needle into my flesh and began his ministrations of sewing me up. What fun.

"What's the *that*?" I asked, gritting my teeth.

"Or that our fathers have all escaped. Someone is helping them, and Kyle was found dead in a kitchen pantry."

"Fuck!" I tensed up.

"You can't do anything. River and Caleb are on their way."

"Which one got stabbed?"

"River. He was coming out of the basement when they were attacked. He took a blade to a shoulder."

"Fuck. Careful," I said.

"You're such a baby."

"Oh, bullshit." I took one last swallow of vodka. With our fathers now out and hiding, I didn't want to be drinking on the job. I was going to be needed to keep Emily safe.

Vadik worked quickly, swiftly, and was putting the finishing touch, complete with a bandage, when River and Caleb came in.

River had already removed his jacket and shirt. Blood dripped from the wound, but it didn't look nasty. Vadik swiped the vodka bottle, handing it to River, who shook his head.

"No, stitch me up," he said.

"You don't have to be a hero."

"I'm not drinking. Not with them out on the loose. Fix me now."

Caleb grabbed the bottle, took a swig, and launched it into the fire. "Fucking pieces of shit."

"So, do you want to tell me what happened?" I asked.

"We believe when Caleb was there last, the camera was hidden and he didn't notice it. He gave them the codes. When Kyle came for his shift, they killed him and busted out our fathers," River said.

"Gave the codes to who, exactly?" I asked.

They all turned toward me.

"Look," I said and took a couple of swallows of vodka, "is anyone curious as to how in the past three years no one has sprung our dads out? It has to be an inside job. There's no way our dads could have gotten word out. Otherwise, this shit would have been a bloodbath a couple of years ago."

River tossed his cell phone to Caleb.

"The only people who went into that fucking basement are us four, Drake, Kyle, and a nurse, Olivia," River said. "But Olivia didn't come for her shift which was today. She was supposed to give them the injections."

"I'm guessing we're going with the nurse then," I said.

"I turn my back for two minutes and you all get injured?" Drake asked. He stood there with a cell phone in his hand.

"You need to get to Emily now!" Caleb said.

Drake turned his cell phone. "I don't. I heard the commotion, but she's sleeping. I admit, it took her a long time to fall asleep. She didn't like me being in her room. I've locked up all of her windows, and there are even wires. I've got everything covered that if anyone gets near her room, I'll know about it. What the fuck happened?"

Caleb gave him the run down. My feelings for this man were still all over the place. I wasn't sure if I completely trusted him, even though he'd proven himself time and again.

He handed his cell phone to Caleb and took River's phone. I watched as he typed away.

"Son of a bitch! She's gone. Olivia suddenly had a big payoff and took off yesterday. Fuck!" He passed the phone to Caleb. "This has soon turned into a shit show, hasn't it?"

"We've got to make her pay," I said. I stood up, but I didn't know if it was the alcohol, lack of food, or the wound that made me feel a little woozy. I quickly sat down. "I'm just going to keep my ass here for the time being."

"We need a plan," River said.

"We brought Emily here and we don't have control," Vadik said. "We need to send her back to England."

"Not happening," Caleb and I said, as did River.

"I'm with these guys, you send her back to England, you may as well slit her throat," Drake said.

"I'm not talking to you."

"I get that none of you like me. I accept it," Drake said. "But I know what I'm doing. Emily's life is in danger, but also yours. You've got four men on the loose who would gladly see you guys rotting in a basement with nowhere else to go. I'm the person who heads up your security, and I warned you guys of this when you started this plan. I'm not going to allow you to push my worries aside. I'd suspected what would play out."

I hated that he was right.

When we'd put our fathers into the basement, Drake had been against the idea. He believed keeping loose ends made for a sloppy way of doing business. I couldn't help but agree with him now.

"Okay, head of security," River said. "What do you propose we do?"

"Your dads, for the past two years have had close to no movement, right?" Drake asked. "The drugs keep them in a catatonic state. They're going to need somewhere to keep a low profile until they can be of sound and mind."

"The drugs don't damage their muscles," Caleb said. "It only numbs them."

"Yeah, but two years of barely using them."

"They've used them at intermittent stages," River said.

I looked at my friends and for once, I actually felt like the sane one. So much so, I couldn't contain my laughter. "You guys have been having little secret visits with our dads. What have you been doing? Training them?"

"Taunting them," Vadik said. "I didn't. I only fed them the drugs, and occasionally told them what our plans were for their empire."

"Me too." I looked at River and Caleb. "Holy shit, you guys have got a cruel streak, and I'm only realizing it now."

"Don't start," Caleb said.

"Come on. They couldn't fight back."

"That was the point," River said. "They needed to know what it was like to experience the kind of pain they put us through."

"I want Earl's number," Caleb said, changing the topic of conversation.

"So, it's okay to talk about my sick mind, but yours, we can't get to it?" I asked.

"We don't have time to point fingers. If Earl didn't betray us, he may have a way of knowing what our fathers are up to. After all, he's the one who made a deal with them first, remember?"

"Yeah, but they didn't exactly give him what he wanted." I pointed out the obvious.

"Exactly." Caleb pointed at me. "While we delivered him a virgin on a silver platter. I have a feeling we can bring Earl to us, get Ashley here, which will put Emily's mind at ease and solve our daddy problem."

"Yeah, I'm going to go and keep an eye on your girl. I have a feeling, after seven years of freedom, this girl is going to go stir-crazy if I'm not careful." Drake got the number for Caleb and then left.

"Do you really think reaching out to Valentine is the right move?" I asked.

"It's a shot, and right now, I'll take anything we can get." He clicked a button on his cell phone and I listened as the call started to ring. I hoped we were making the right decision.

Chapter Eleven

Vadik

A couple of hours later

I plunged the spoon into the ice cream and took a large bite. The shock of the cold hurt my teeth, but at the moment, I needed to feel something. Between River's and Gael's wounds, the revelation of what River and Caleb did, our dads being on the loose, along with the attackers, I was tired. I needed ice cream.

No, I needed Emily, but right now, I didn't want her to panic, and I didn't know if I could keep control of all the shit swirling in my head. There was a lot to process. A lot going on, and I had to get my shit together.

"You're still awake?" Emily asked, as if my thoughts had magically made her appear.

"You should be asleep."

"I woke up. Needed some water, but ice cream sometimes works."

I offered the spoon and she came close to me.

"You don't look happy," she said.

"I'm not." I didn't want to lie to her, which was another reason I wanted to avoid her.

"Do you want to talk about it?"

"No."

"Okay."

I looked at her, waiting for the questions to start. They didn't. All she did was dip the spoon into the tub and start to eat. Her tongue came out, licking the bottom of the spoon.

"You're not curious?"

"You know I am," she said. "But I also know what it's like to just want to be alone with my thoughts. I'm guessing something big went down, didn't it?"

"Yeah, it did."

"You also want to protect me."

"Always."

"You'll tell me if you feel I need to know." She cupped my face, rubbing her thumb back and forth.

"You know, the last seven years were the hardest of our lives," I said.

"I know."

"We only did what we had to in order to protect you."

She licked her lips and I saw the tears shining in her eyes. I didn't want to make her cry.

"I get it, Vadik, I do."

I stared at her. There was no judgment, no anger, no resentment. It was like she was a different person. Whatever Drake had said to her, it had given her a new perspective.

"We fucked up."

This made her pause in eating her ice cream. "What do you mean?"

I pressed my lips together, fighting with the decision of if I should tell her or not. It wasn't going to do either of us any good, and finally, I decided to tell her.

"Your life is in danger." I told her everything. I told her about the dads' escape, the attackers, and the call to Earl Valentine. "He's coming here. He's bringing Ashley with him. So long as we don't take her from him, he's going to help us. He wants to settle an old score with them. They made promises to him that they didn't keep."

"Wait." Emily held her hand up. "Ashley's coming here?"

"Yes."

"You're going to let him leave with her."

I took her hands, kissing each of her knuckles. "We're going to do everything we can to save her. I promise."

She breathed out a sigh of relief. "Wow, no wonder you're eating ice cream."

"I didn't want to tell you."

She chuckled. "Oops."

"I don't like keeping secrets from you."

"Good. I'm glad." This time, she kissed my hands. "I don't like you keeping secrets from me either." She took a deep breath. "So, Ashley is coming here and there are at least five people who want me dead."

"No, four."

She smiled. "If you killed an attacker, as did River and Caleb, that means there is at least one more on the loose."

Before I had a chance to speak, one of the soldiers crashed through the door. Gunshots rang out, and I quickly dived to my woman, getting her to the floor as the man who'd just taken out at least one of our men charged forward. I didn't recognize him, but I knew the sort of man he was. A trained killer, hired to do a job. Our dads weren't wasting any time. I kicked the gun out of his hand, sending my fist into his gut, which made him bend, giving me the perfect shot in the face. He blocked the punch, shoving me back hard. I was off-balance as he slammed me into the counter. It would all sting in the morning.

I wasn't one to go down lightly. Grabbing him around the neck, I took him down with me. We knocked chairs to the floor. He hit me twice in the face, and the third time I head-butted him, it was so hard I saw stars.

Emily screamed my name. There was no way I could let this bastard get to her.

The gun went off and the man grunted. He head-butted me twice until I let him go. Dazed, he climbed off me and I heard more than one gunshot ring out. Getting to my feet, I saw our attacker was on the floor. Emily pressed a hand to her shoulder, blood seeping through her fingers.

I went to her as Gael, Drake, River, and Caleb each appeared in the kitchen.

"We need a doctor!" I put my hand over her wound, hating that I'd failed her. I'd never been bested in a fight and this was a harsh reality to deal with. Drake tossed his cell phone at River, going toward the dead body.

"I'm fine," Emily said.

She swayed a little on her feet. Picking her up in my arms, I carried her through to the sitting room, putting her down gently on the sofa. She pulled her hand away and winced. "Ugh, it hurts."

"What the fuck happened?"

"We were attacked on our own land. One of our men is already dead, and Em's hurt. Can't you see what's going on?" I tore at Emily's pajama shirt to expose her wound. It looked clean, it was just bleeding profusely. After removing my shirt, I wrapped it around her, tightening it as best as I could.

"Your dads are moving fast," she said. "Do you think he was a hired killer or just a desperate man?"

"He was hired," I said. "There's no way anyone could be that strong without some training. The son of a bitch knew what he was doing." I didn't like that I wasn't able to win that fight. If Emily didn't know how to handle a gun, she would've been dead. I hated that I couldn't protect her.

"The doctor's on his way," River said, coming into the room.

"You don't have to worry," she said. "It's just a bullet wound."

"You shouldn't have been shot," Caleb said.

I gritted my teeth, standing up. I grabbed the vase closest to me and launched it across the room.

"Vadik." Emily went to grab my arm, but I pulled away.

"I don't know what's going on," Gael asked.

"I couldn't protect her." I yelled the words, letting them fill the room, echoing off the walls. I couldn't stand that I was weak.

Emily wrapped her arms around me. "Stop it."

"You need to rest." I didn't feel like I deserved her love. I was useless to her.

"Vadik, stop it."

"I'm not good enough."

She squeezed me tighter. "I said stop it, and I mean it. Do not think I won't kick your ass, even with a gunshot wound. You did everything you could to save me. He took us by surprise. Anyone would have struggled in your position. We're both alive. Don't do this."

I couldn't help it. I still felt like I'd fucked up.

She spun me around, cupping my face and drawing me down to kiss my lips. Wrapping my arms around her, I pressed my face against her neck, breathing her in. I wouldn't fail her again.

****

Emily

The following day

"I'm bored."

"Then get unbored," Drake said.

He was my company until all threats were removed. I didn't like it. After I put one of my cards down on the pile, Drake immediately put his down.

Throwing the rest of the cards down, I stood up. "I don't want to play." I moved toward the library window, pushing some of my hair out of my eyes. All I wanted was for Ashley to get here.

Caleb, River, Gael, and Vadik were out. All of them on the hunt for their fathers. Crude Hill wasn't exactly a big town, but it sure had a lot of places to hide. They wanted me dead and from what little information I'd gotten, this went beyond ignoring their orders. I didn't like it.

I hated that they were in danger because of me. Letting out a breath, I shoved my hands into my jeans and looked out across the gardens. The last seven years, I'd been able to come and go as I pleased. Now I'd been ordered to stay inside the house. The same house I'd nearly been killed inside.

"Where do you think they are?" I asked.

Out of all of the men in my life, Drake was the only one willing not to treat me like a baby, and he was the only one I wasn't in a relationship with.

"If I was them, I'd go to a place I knew my sons wouldn't look."

I glanced back to see Drake shuffling the cards.

"Come on, I'll let you win."

"I don't like cheating. I can play just as good as you."

"Then prove it. Stop behaving like a girl."

"You know, I don't like you," I said.

"Don't care."

I stepped toward the table and threw the cards across the room. "Now they're shuffled."

"You're a child, you know that?"

I rolled my eyes. "I don't need to be here." I rushed toward the door, charged out, and ran down toward the door. I didn't get far before Drake was on me, his arms around my body. He was too strong. Even as I wriggled, he didn't let me go. "Get off me."

"You're being a very naughty girl and I'm growing tired of this."

Before I knew what was happening, he had me thrown across his shoulder and he was carrying me upstairs. I didn't think about safety as I punched his ass and the backs of his legs. At one point, I thought I even bit him.

For my trouble, he slapped me hard.

"I'm going to make them gut you. No one is going to ever recognize you, not even in hell. Let me go."

I entered a room and within a matter of seconds, he had me tied to a bedpost. Then I felt something click around my neck.

"What the hell?"

Drake sighed. "I think the beating I'll get for this is worth it."

I glared at him. "You're not funny."

"I don't claim to be funny, but you sure look sexy as fuck with my chains on you." His arms were folded. "It's a shame I don't see you as anything more than a pain in the ass and my bosses' woman. You look nice chained up."

"You're sick." It gave me some relief knowing he wasn't trying to get into my pants.

"No, I'm natural."

I glared at him again but decided to look around the room. "Is this your room?"

"Yep. I live here with the bosses. I'm damn good at what I do. I do have my own place, but I don't see a reason letting women think they have a chance with me other than a quick fuck."

"You're disgusting."

He winked at me and for some reason, it pissed me off.

"They're going to cut your balls off for this."

"Probably, but when I tell them it was this or chasing you outside where all those nasty assassins are, I think this one will work. They don't need to be worrying about you. While you're with me, they're focused on not dying."

"The loyalty act is getting old. You're not fooling me."

"Good, I'm not trying to fool anyone." He sighed and sat down in a chair. "Soon, your legs are going to get tired, and your arms. I've made sure you can't move more than an inch. Not enough to sit or to get comfortable."

"And woman want to do this for you?"

"I have all my women screaming in orgasms. Believe me, Emily, I know what I do brings women to their knees, and they'd gladly do whatever I ask them. I'm a master."

"Why is your loyalty so real?" I wanted to trip him up and to find a weak spot. There was no way this man was loyal to mine. I just didn't see it. I'd been out of the loop for a while, but that didn't mean people changed so dramatically.

"You're not very trusting."

"High school."

"I was there. What about it?" He pressed a palm to his mouth, faking a yawn.

"I remember what you were like. You were nothing but a tantruming baby."

"So? You have yet to tell me something I don't know."

"Why are you suddenly their best friend?" I asked.

"I've told you the reason I am the way I am. You don't believe me. I'm not going to keep justifying my existence in their world. I've done my time, proven myself. What about you?"

"What about me?"

"What exactly have you ever done to have the loyalty of those men? As far as I can tell, you've done fuck all."

"Fuck you."

"No thanks, sweetheart, you're not my type."

I wanted to throw something at him. He wasn't wrong. My arms had already started to get tired and he was pissing me off. I had a feeling he was doing this on purpose. He liked to torture me.

"You're a dick."

He got up out of his chair. "Go on then, princess. Tell me what exactly it is you've done."

I stared at him. "You don't know what I did?"

"Enlighten me."

"I killed for them. I saved Gael from death. That's what I did."

"And now?"

"Now, nothing has changed."

"You've changed, Emily. You just can't see it. You're too blinded by your love to see how much you have, but whatever, it's not my place to fix you. Are you hungry?"

"What the hell do you mean?"

"Is your stomach hurting and you need food?"

"That's not what I meant and you know it." I wanted to kill him. "I mean about me. What you said."

"It's not my place, and frankly, I don't want to help you."

"Just tell me. If not for me, then for them. Will that work?" I asked. I refused to beg him for help. I didn't put it past him to try, though.

He stared at me for several seconds. "In high

school, whatever you guys had, you knew it wasn't going to last. Before it became anything real, you were gone. Now your men are kings, and they're expecting you to be a queen. You know this life and you know that life. Which one do you want? We both know there's only one outcome here. Will you hurt my boys, or make the sacrifice?"

He was gone and since I didn't have a choice, I paused, shocked.

Drake was right. I knew the freedom of not being part of this world. Of not having assassins at my door. Of being completely free. Could I give up a life of safety to be with my men? Did I even want to?

Gael, Caleb, Vadik, and River, none of them could give this up. This was their life. I couldn't ask them to, but did I want to be a queen of such an empire?

Chapter Twelve

Gael

I was tired.

Hungry.

Pissed off.

And thirsty for blood.

As I entered our house, the soldiers we'd put in place immediately disappeared. I paused as I heard soft music filtering the house.

Caleb, Vadik, and River stood frozen.

I couldn't recall the last time I'd heard such soft and beautiful music. It was so sad and full of passion. Without going to get cleaned up, I followed the sound, opening doors to find the rooms empty.

The house was too fucking large. I hadn't wanted to live in any of our fathers' houses, but I knew the statement we were making was by far more important. Like now, we always had to consider our reputation.

I came to a stop with my friends and we looked into the main dining room that also had a dance floor and a piano. I stay perfectly still, watching as Drake played the tune and Emily sang as she danced around the dining room. There were no table or chairs since we'd had them removed. We didn't intend to entertain and with each new threat happening, we didn't want anything that could cause us a hindrance.

She spun around. I didn't recognize the song, but it sounded so sad. Her voice wasn't great, but she clearly didn't care. Over and over, Drake played the same tune, and not once did Emily stop in her singing.

The last note was played and Emily came to a stop. Her head tilted to the sky, her hands clenched into fists. The silence almost heartbreaking after such beauty.

Caleb stepped into the room and the floor creaked.

Emily opened her eyes and spun around. The instant she saw us, she burst out laughing and rushed to all of us. Caleb got her first, lifting her up in his arms and spinning her around.

Drake put the lid down on the piano. "You didn't find them?"

"No," Caleb said.

Drake nodded. "You're going to want to beat me up."

"No," Emily said. "They're not. It's all fine. Just a misunderstanding. Are you guys hungry?"

"Starved," River said.

"Come on. Drake made us dinner earlier." She rushed out of the room. Drake started to follow her, but I couldn't help but grab his arm.

"No," I said.

"What the hell are you telling me no to?" Drake asked. "You don't want me to go and follow your woman? Don't want me to cook?"

"You don't get to fall in love with her."

He threw his head back and laughed. I clenched my hand into a fist.

"I hate to break it to you, Gael. She's not my type. I'm not in love with your woman, nor do I ever want your woman. Back in high school, I thought she had a stick up her ass. My feelings about her haven't changed. I've got your guys' backs, but it doesn't mean I want to compete with my dick, got it?"

"Good. Make sure it stays that way."

I let him go and followed close behind him. Emily was in the dining room. She'd laid out our plates for us. The food smelled good.

"Drake made pie. It's really good." She took a

seat next to me as Vadik and River sat opposite. Caleb took the head of the table. After picking up my fork, I had a mouthful, and when that didn't kill me I ate some more.

I stared at Drake.

"Well, if you don't need me I'll go and get some sleep." He got to his feet and left.

Emily watched him go.

"If you want me to kill him, I will."

"No, don't be silly. He's an ass, but he doesn't deserve to die. Tell me how today went."

I took another forkful of food. We hadn't had a good day. First of all, at the edge of our property, one of our men had been held in a bear trap. There was a chance he might lose his leg, which pissed me off. Our men were dropping like flies.

Our fathers weren't wasting a second in letting us know they were a threat.

"It's going good," Caleb said.

"Don't do that. Don't shut me out. I might be able to help."

"The only way you can help us right now is by staying inside and not leaving this house," Caleb said.

She tensed up. "I should have known you wouldn't trust me with all of this."

"Emily, I'm not being a dick to you. It's dangerous."

"And you think I don't get that? I do. I promise I do." She sighed and ran fingers through her hair. She looked pissed off.

Even though my hands were dirty, I took hold of hers, locking our fingers together, so she knew I was with her. I didn't want to lose her.

She squeezed me back.

"It's dangerous out there." Crude Hill had always

been filled with hell. Even the school. Our lives had only been worth as much as our parents were willing to sacrifice for it.

After running a hand down my face, I finished up the food and pushed my plate away.

"I'm going to take a shower." I let go of Emily.

I hated this.

We'd built this empire, rivaling our fathers', and now they had us chasing after them. Emily's life was constantly in danger and it pissed me off.

I wasn't a happy man.

After going to my bedroom, I went straight to the bathroom, stripping off my clothes and stepping beneath the cold bathroom spray. I tilted my head back, letting out a sigh as the water cascaded all over my body.

This was what I wanted.

Eyes closed, I sensed her.

I didn't know how I could, but I knew the moment she entered my bathroom, then my shower. I turned to watch her. She was naked. Her hands were crossed over her chest, trying to hide those glorious tits from me.

"I thought you could use some company."

As I held my hand out, she took it and came closer to me. Body to body, I pressed my face against her neck, breathing her in. She was the only woman I wanted. The instant I held her, the beast within me calmed. She was here, flesh and blood, and we were going to protect her. I did believe that.

Her fingers teased at the base of my neck.

"I'm here, Gael."

"I love you, Emily."

She pulled back, staring into my eyes. "I love you too. So much it scares me. I don't … what if I'm not good enough for you? What if you do all of this and I can't, I can't be the woman you want?"

"Not going to happen."

She went to protest and I silenced her with a kiss.

Both of her arms went around the back of my neck. Sliding my hands down to her ass, I cupped the flesh, hearing her moan. My cock was already rock-hard and I wanted inside her. Spinning her around to the wall, I lifted her, using the wall as leverage to keep her in place. I reached between us, gripping my cock, lining it up at her entrance, and sank her onto my length. Her cries filled the air as I started to fuck her.

I went slow, feeling every inch of her cunt wrapped around my cock, but when I couldn't wait another moment, I fucked her harder. The angle was all wrong. Pulling out, I spun her around so she was bent over. Holding on to her hips, I found my way back inside her and wildly drove inside her, fucking her harder than ever before.

"Fuck, Emily. You have no idea what you do to me."

"I'm getting an idea."

Over and over, I pounded her pussy, taking what I wanted.

Just as my orgasm started to take over, I remembered I hadn't brought her to orgasm. I held her tightly against me as I spilled within her walls. With my cock still balls deep inside her, I reached between her thighs and stroked her clit, feeling her pussy tighten around me.

I wanted to lick her pussy, but I also didn't want to stop since I loved how she responded to being on my cock.

Over and over, I teased her clit, drawing her closer to her orgasm. When she went over, I closed my eyes, basking in the tightness wrapped around my dick.

This was what I loved, and I wasn't going to give it up, not for a second. She was perfect in every single way. Our dads had better watch out, because I was coming for them.

****

Caleb

I didn't expect to find Emily in her bedroom, but there she was, sitting in the middle of her bed, book in hand. She'd followed Gael, so I thought she'd be with him.

"Hey," she said.

"Hey. Ashley and Earl should be here tomorrow."

"Great."

"You're not with Gael?"

"I…" She frowned. "I don't exactly know how all of this works. I'm kind of new to more than one boyfriend. I don't want to upset anyone." She ran fingers through her still damp hair. "You all know that I've had sex with you. Admitted I love River and Gael, and now you."

"You love me?"

She laughed. "Yes, I love you. I love you all. And Vadik. When I woke up seven years ago, I hated that I wouldn't get the chance to tell you all that I loved you. I promised myself if I ever got the chance to tell you all how I felt, I'd take it. Only, it came and went, and I didn't take it. I do love you all. This is so fucked up."

I closed the door and moved toward the bed, sitting on the edge. "Why is it?"

"Because it is. How is it going to work? We haven't even talked about protection and we've had sex. Each time we have sex, the risk of having a baby is higher. How is that going to work?"

"Isn't it working now?"

"You're all going to share me and I get passed around while you all have sex with me?" she asked.

"You only go with the four of us. It's not like I'm going to let the soldiers have a chance at you."

She wrinkled her nose. "But what happens when you get bored? Or I get tired? Or you don't want to wait your turn?"

"Em, you're overthinking all of this."

"Am I? You guys are willing to share, but what if one of you takes me more than the other?" She blew out a breath. "I think I'm giving myself a headache."

"We don't want rules or charts, Em. I don't want to start putting dates down on a calendar of who can get you when. That's not going to work. We all want you."

"And if you want me at the same time?"

"I had no problem watching you with Gael. I like to watch."

Her frown deepened. "And when it no longer works?"

I moved a little closer so I could tuck a stray curl behind her ear. "It's going to work."

"But what if it doesn't?"

"It won't not work, purely because you've got all of us working together. We're going to make this happen, Em."

She licked her lips. "I'm sorry. You've probably got more important information to deal with, don't you?"

"I don't mind. It's nice not thinking about all the other stuff."

Emily took my hand, locking our fingers together. "Everyone looks to you, don't they? You can't take a step back."

"I wouldn't want to. Every empire needs a leader. That's me. I know how to listen to my friends."

She nodded. "You can't find your fathers."

"No." I blew out a breath. "I don't know where to fucking look. It pisses me off. I've tried all the motels and hotels. They're going to want somewhere comfortable to gain their strength back."

"What if you've got that wrong?" she asked.

"How do you mean?" I knew our parents. They were used to a life of luxury. It was why our punishment was so fucking perfect. We took everything away from them that they ever loved. It was cruel but fun. I enjoyed every second of it, knowing they were never going to know a moment's peace. However, I hadn't foreseen them getting out. Drake had. He'd warned us that permanently keeping them alive came with risks.

I figured we'd taken care of all of our dads' allies. I hadn't expected Olivia to betray us. I already had men capturing her and bringing her back here to face the consequences.

"Your dads know you all better than anyone, so they will also know what you'd do next. What if they're in places you wouldn't expect them? I don't know, rundown apartments. Did they have any places in their estate? Maybe places that you wouldn't think to look."

I frowned. "They're going to want comfort."

"Not if it's going to lead you all to them. They want to take over, right? They're your enemy now. They're going to try and take you out, one by one."

I got to my feet, rushing from her room.

All I wanted tonight was to hold her. I wasn't going to lie, getting my dick wet would have been even better, but I'd settle for holding her.

With what Emily said, it made sense.

"Caleb?" she asked, following behind me.

I went straight to my office. Emily closed the door as I pulled the painting off the wall and revealed my safe. After putting in the code, I opened it up and pulled out a my father's portfolio. My dad was the one who kept all the necessary details of land, buildings, and stocks the Monsters had required. I thought I'd been through all of this, but it had been a few years. Flicking the file open, I saw the deeds to the main houses they possessed. They even owned the land the school was built on. That wasn't a surprise to me. The school helped to shape soldiers and the next generation.

There were land purchases all over the country, warehouses, and I came to a stop at an apartment building.

It was on the edge of town, surrounded by a woodland. I pointed my finger at it, handing it over to Emily. "There!"

"You're sure?"

"I overlooked it. It's a piece-of-shit apartment building. It wasn't finished due to some subsidence, I think. I can't remember all the details. I just recall it being useless. They've got to be there. Everywhere else, I've got eyes and ears." I laughed. Cupping Emily's face, I pulled her close. "You're a genius."

"Caleb, they might not be there."

"I don't care." I kissed her again. "I've got to get the boys up."

"Caleb, don't go tonight."

"Not happening. I'm going to handle this now. I'm not having you afraid."

"But I'm not afraid and you're tired."

"Trust me."

I left the office and went to Gael's, Vadik's, and River's rooms, waking them up.

Emily was still following me around. I got changed in my room, grabbing my favorite guns and putting them within easy reach.

"I don't like this," Emily said.

My friends were waiting at the front door as I came downstairs. Drake was there. "You stay with her. Keep her here, do you understand me?"

He nodded. "I don't like this."

"I know that's where they're going to be."

"Then send soldiers to do some recon. We don't know what kind of backup your fathers have. We don't know their power."

"They don't have any because we've taken it all." Caleb laughed. "This ends tonight and as soon as it does, we'll be able to handle Valentine. I'm doing this for you, Emily."

I kissed her again and headed out into the night where a van was already waiting to take me away.

Climbing into the car, Gael jumped into the front seat. "You're not acting out of your ass, are you?"

"No. We can't find them, and we all know what our fathers are like. Emily is right. They're going to be in places we wouldn't think to look."

"I hope you're right. I don't want to be indebted to Valentine when the truth is I want to fucking kill him."

"After we've made him pay," I said.

"Of course."

I smiled. Tonight, we would end this. I could already feel the sweet sense of victory.

Chapter Thirteen

Emily

I rushed toward the door, but they were already on their way. The car lights already disappearing.

"Get inside," Drake said.

I was getting pissed off with being left alone with him. He wasn't exactly my favorite person to spend time with. "Stop ordering me around."

"Don't get pissed with me because your men go off half-cocked."

I wanted to slap him, but instead, I just glared at him as I stepped away from the door. He rolled his eyes at me and then before I even realized what I was doing, I put my hand out as if to slap him.

He caught me before it even landed.

"You want to fight, I'm all for it, but I don't let anyone off easy, little girl. You should know that." He pushed me away but I was able to keep my footing.

"You've got to go and stop them."

"No can do. I can't do anything that they don't want me to."

"I bet you can. You're just choosing to be difficult."

He sighed. "I've got strict orders."

"And I've told you to go after them."

"You don't pay me."

I growled, and feeling even more like a child rather than a grown woman, I stormed off toward the back of the house, only I stopped at the library.

Rather than go to my room, I stepped inside. The scent of books flooded my senses. I used to love the library when I was a teenager. Especially while I waited for my driver. It was the one place I felt completely safe.

No one could get me here.

Stepping into the room, I flicked on the light.

I know Drake wouldn't be too far. He'd become my own personal shadow, and it pissed me off. I knew deep down he was only doing what my men wanted of him, but what about me?

They'd taken me from my old home, and it seemed at each opportunity, they abandoned me. Sure, there was a huge threat to my life, but still, wouldn't they want to spend what time they could with me before I died? I reached out and touched the spine of one of the books. It hadn't been read, and I slid it out, not recognizing the title. It looked like a really old title, maybe even a first edition.

If this was Caleb's dad's collection, then I would understand him doing nothing with these books other than using them for display pieces. All of them.

Running my fingers through my hair, I hummed to myself as I continued to touch unread spines.

None of them were read. All for show.

Coming to a stop at a giant globe, I smiled at the pretentiousness of everything. The classic-looking family library but never used. I wondered how many people would have appreciated this room and yet no one else could because it was locked up in this house.

After several minutes, I'd lost the feeling of someone watching me, which was nice. Drake knew how to do that. He wouldn't be far.

When I heard some movement in the stacks on the floor above, I paused.

No one else should be here. This was a private room. Going to the fire, which looked like it had never been lit, I grabbed a metal poker, gripping it in my hands as I started to move up the steps, going toward the stacks. More unread books. More pretense.

The sound of movement made me stop.

Someone was in the stacks.

My heart raced and my hands shook. I held the poker even tighter. I didn't make a sound.

I'd always hated it in movies when it came to a scary or tense part where the hero or heroine, or any one of the characters would call out *hello*, or *who is there*. Yeah, it pissed me off. Everyone always knew someone was there, and most of the time, it wasn't good. My stomach turned as possibilities grew.

I wouldn't give away where I was or what I had.

Patience.

A sound on my right had me turning. Nothing there.

Someone knew these bookshelves, and it wasn't me. There were only four people I knew who would be able to get into this house undetected and be familiar with these bookcases. Holy shit. I turned on my heel and rushed back to the steps. As I reached the top step, I felt the hands at my back shove me hard. I released the poker as I cried out, falling down the steps, hitting my head as I went.

Once I reached the ground, I was thoroughly winded. I groaned at the sudden jolt to my entire body. This wasn't good.

Opening my eyes, I attempted to scurry away from the attacker. I was shocked to see Ace Block standing before me.

He wasn't as big as I remembered, but the demons within his gaze were exactly the same as the last time I saw him.

"So, they finally brought you back, you little slut."

I grunted, feeling pain explode as he landed a blow with his foot to my stomach.

Where the fuck was Drake? I couldn't believe I even wanted him here to save me, but I was no match for this man. He was dangerous.

Rolling over, I ignored each sparkle of pain and got to my feet, only to have a blow across the cheek. He didn't hit me with an open palm but a fist so hard, I saw stars. Not good. Really, not good.

I fell against the table and in my hand, I found some kind of box. With my weapon, I spun around when I felt him close, and lashed out, hitting him over the head. He took a step back, but it wasn't enough to take him out. Still with the box in my hand, I went in for the attack again. He caught my hand, twisting it so I had no choice but to drop my weapon. I lifted my foot to try to stomp on him, to kick him, to do anything that would free me.

He pushed me away and I fell into a cabinet.

More pain exploded throughout my body. It had been a long time since I'd taken a beating, and I was starting to feel it, and what was more, I didn't like it.

As I turned to try to block him, I wasn't fast enough. He grabbed my head, holding me up by my hair until I cried out. I couldn't stand the pain and I knew he was going to rip chunks of hair right out of my head.

Tears exploded in my eyes.

"Fucker!"

Never had I been so relieved to hear Drake's voice. I heard him hit Ace and the tightness of my hair loosened.

Dropping to the floor, I turned and tried to scurry away, but my leg was captured and I was pulled back. Ace had me and his fingers were wrapped around my neck, cutting off my air supply.

The movement was so quick, I couldn't stop it. I tried to claw at his arms, to get him to release me.

Nothing. I couldn't stop him.

He was the one in charge.

Where was Drake?

I hadn't been able to spend enough time with Gael, Caleb, Vadik, and River. I didn't want to die without at least being with them long enough to appreciate it. I'd been too pissed about everything to be happy to be with them.

Suddenly, out of the corner of my eye, I saw Drake with a knife. Ace was so focused on me that he didn't hear Drake, who was sporting a gash across his forehead.

Within seconds, Drake embedded his knife into Ace's throat. Blood spilled out and I tried to turn away, but I felt it drip down onto my face and neck.

I gasped, hoping I didn't get any blood into my mouth.

Ace's weight was off me and I rolled over, going to my knees and taking large gulps of breath.

"One down, three to go," Drake said. "Fuck."

"Where were you?" I croaked the words out, my hand going to my throat. I glanced toward the door and saw a tray of food spilled to the floor. "Oh."

"I was trying to get you something to eat. I'm going to need a fucking assistant. I'm not letting you out of my sight." Drake grabbed my arm and helped me up. "Are you okay?"

"I'm alive. I'll take that for now. I'm alive."

Ace's body was on the floor.

Drake hadn't pulled the knife out, and the man lay completely lifeless.

"Do you need me to move it for you?"

"No, I'm fine. I don't need to be protected like that. I can handle it."

"You sure?"

"I'm sure. Believe me." My voice didn't sound like mine, and my throat still felt so incredibly tight. I let out a little cough, hoping to clear my throat, but nothing. Drake put a finger beneath my chin and tilted my head back.

"You're going to have bruises."

"Yay."

We were still sitting on the sofa hours later when my men returned empty-handed. Their search had been completely useless, which I had suspected. Rather than be pissed at them leaving me alone, I went to them. They were angry and they all held me. I didn't want to let them go, but eventually, we walked over to the corpse of Ace Block.

I glanced at River, but he wasn't showing any emotion at all.

He didn't seem to care.

I wondered if they even realized that Ace had been in this house before they'd left, and we hadn't known it. It made me wonder where the other three were because I had a feeling they were a lot closer than was comfortable.

****

River

"I'm fine. Really," Emily said.

"Don't care." I had a pillow. Gael, Caleb, and Vadik are already camped out in Emily's bedroom, and I joined them. Her bed was big enough to take us all, but some mattresses had been pulled into the room around her bed.

Caleb sat on the bed, as did Vadik. Gael sat on one of the mattresses, cleaning one of his guns. I'd never been a fan of guns. I much preferred the clean cut of a blade.

"You want us to go?" I asked.

"No, of course not, but I don't want you to stick around if you don't want to."

I laughed. I couldn't help it. She didn't want us to leave, but she was also nervous about asking us to stay. She was so cute.

Climbing onto the bed, I touched her ankle. Bruises had already started to appear on her flesh.

I glanced up her body. Marks were on her legs, and I'd already caught sight of the ones across her stomach and chest.

Finger marks dotted her neck, and she had a cut across her eyebrow, as well as a swollen cheek. My dad should have suffered.

When we'd arrived at the empty apartment building, we discovered subsidence had taken effect and part of the structure had already crumbled down. When we'd gone there years ago, there had been a large split within the walls. We'd decided, as an investment, it had been useless and we'd wait to see where the natural fall of the land happened. There was no reason to pull down the building. It was tightly restricted and guarded. The men we paid had been there waiting. There had been no signs of movement. I'd known we wouldn't catch our dads.

They were clearly much better at the game of hide-and-seek than we were.

After running a hand down my face, I crawled across the bed and wrapped my arms around her waist as I put my face onto her lap.

"I'm fine, River. You don't have to worry about me."

"I'm never going to stop worrying about you." I rubbed my face against her. Letting her go had been the hardest thing I'd ever done, but living with her dead, I couldn't do that. I wasn't strong enough to do that.

She ran her fingers through my hair. I closed my eyes, basking in her touch.

"I'm here, River. I'm alive."

Her voice was croaky from being strangled. "We shouldn't have left you."

"Now you know where they're not."

"You don't understand, Emily," Caleb said. "If they're not in any of their usual places, or even in old buildings they owned, where are they?"

Silence met Caleb's question.

"Have you ever thought that maybe they're here?" Emily asked.

I lifted my head. Gael had finished cleaning his gun and joined us.

"What?"

"Well, Ace was here. No one detected him and Drake went and did a sweep when you guys arrived. No soldiers were killed. He got inside this house undetected."

"Because he knows this house," Caleb said.

"Do you guys know this house?"

I looked toward Caleb, who stared at each of us.

"I'm starting to think we don't know it as well as we could."

"We could get the blueprints," Vadik said. "It would give us a clear picture of every single part of the house."

"I'll call up the architect," Caleb said.

Emily reached out, putting a hand over his. "Not tonight," she said.

"Em, baby, every second I waste puts you in danger."

"Drake killed one of their own tonight. I imagine if they are close, they know what happened. They're brothers, like you, right? They will want to mourn the death of their friend. At least for tonight." She breathed out a sigh. "Besides, there is something I want to talk to you guys about, and I think it's important."

"Is this about Ashley?" Vadik asked.

"No. I'm looking forward to seeing her."

I sat up and she smiled at all of us. "I should probably just get this over with and you know, just deal." She breathed out a sigh. "Okay, so, we all have a history together. We've been through a lot."

"Em, where are you going with this?" Caleb asked.

"Seriously, let her fucking speak," Gael shot back.

I chuckled at the sudden death glare Caleb sent Gael. If we all shut up, Emily could get to whatever was on her mind.

"You all speak about me being your woman. I don't know how this is going to work. If this even can work. There are four of you, and I've told you all that I love you."

We all spoke at the same time, telling her how we felt that we loved her as well. I did, more than anything in the world. I loved her so damn much it scared me.

"I know," Emily said. "But, I'm only me. I'm one person. I'm not some magical woman that you can split down into three or four of me. What if you grow tired of me?"

"Not going to happen, Em," I said. My friends agreed.

"You say that now, but people change."

"You're right, people do change," Caleb said. "But we're not like other people. Sharing you is all we want to do. I'm not interested in any other woman."

"Anyone else could have saved Gael," she said.

I chuckled. "It's not just about Gael." I touched her ankle. "You feel that. The rush? We all get that by being near you. Seven years and I'm not going to lie to you, Em, we did shit that embarrasses us. Some of us did try to use other women in a way to forget you, but I speak for all of us when I say we weren't able to go all the way. Kissing them, holding them, even thinking about fucking them, was a betrayal to you. All we want is you, and we're willing to make this work. You as our woman. We don't want lists, or charts, or schedules. We only want what is natural, which is you with us."

"No jealousy?"

"None," I said.

"We're very good at sharing," Gael said.

"However," Caleb said.

I turned toward him, wondering what the fuck he was doing throwing a wrench in the works. We didn't need a *however*, or any fucking *but* coming along.

"We all know you've experienced a life without us. Without being hit or scared for your life. We all get it and we know it's a lot to ask for you to stay with us. To take a chance on us." He sighed. "If you don't want to live this life, be our queen, then you've got this one chance to tell us. When the danger is over, we'll take you back to your life, far away from us, where you don't even have to think about us. We'd make sure you want for nothing and live in peace and happiness."

Okay, what the fuck? It was all right for Caleb to offer this, but I didn't want that. I sure as fuck didn't want to lose her.

We'd only just gotten her and now he was talking about letting her go. I didn't see a future without her in it. I refused to see any kind of life without her in it.

"You'd let me go?"

"Yes."

"But, doesn't that go against your feelings?"

Hell, yeah! I kept it to myself. Caleb was clearly working on an idea, even if I did think it was completely stupid. Asshole.

"It does. I didn't say it would be easy to let you go, Emily. I'm offering you a chance because the moment you agree to stay with us and make a life here with us, none of us are ever letting you go. I can't let you go. I don't want to."

She licked her lips and I saw tears in her eyes once again. I was getting tired of us hurting her like this. It wasn't exactly fair of us.

"So, er, what you're saying is, if I stay, I'll be by your side for the rest of my life?"

"Yes. You'll marry one of us," Caleb said. "Probably me, but you'd be married to all of us, Em."

She smiled. "You know, I wondered about this. I thought I wanted my old life back in England. The peace and quiet, but while I was there, all I wanted was to be here." She sank her teeth into her lip. "I could have died tonight and when he had his fingers wrapped around my neck, all I wanted to do was live." She looked up. "All I want in my life is to be with you guys. I don't know what it is you do to me, but I don't want to be anywhere else. This is home. With you guys. I still don't think it's the perfect setup, but if you want me, then I want you all so much."

"Then we're going to make it work," I said.

"Fuck, yeah," Gael said.

"I like that Caleb gave you the illusion of having a choice," Vadik said.

Emily laughed, resting her head on his shoulder. "I love you all. All of you crazy, stupid men."

"We're stupid, crazy in love with you," Gael said.

She shook her head. "That's not good. What do

you guys think about kids?"

"Love them," I said, and I did. I wanted a whole load of kids, but I had a feeling Caleb wasn't so fond of the idea, especially after what happened to his mom.

"I want them," Gael said.

"Me too," Vadik said.

Caleb was silent.

"It's a lot to take in," she said.

"We'll make it work," Caleb said. "We all will make this work."

Chapter Fourteen

Vadik

Ashley and Earl were due to arrive any time now. They didn't exactly give us a time for when they would be here, just a day. Emily stood in the closet, a towel wrapped around her body as she fingered her way through the endless supply of dresses, skirts, pants, and shirts. We'd fully stocked her closet.

I was distracted by the small gap in the towel that kept showing off an impressive, juicy thigh. Emily had lost weight during her time away from us, and I hated it because I knew it was down to sadness. When Emily finally fell asleep last night, we all agreed to do our part in taking care of her. We weren't going to fail her again.

She was the love of our life in every single way that counted. We were going to make this work, and part of that was taking out our family once and for all.

I never wanted Emily to know the truth of the extent of torture I put my father through, just for the pleasure of it. He'd hurt me and I had gone out of my way to hurt him. If I didn't find him first, I knew it was going to cost me in a big way. He'd hurt Emily and I couldn't allow that to happen.

"I have no idea what to wear," she said, taking out a black dress, which looked a little too formal to me.

"She's your best friend, right?"

"Yes, of course."

"Then why not just go with the whole casual look?"

She groaned. "We haven't seen each other in so long."

"Emily, babe, it has been about a week."

This made her stop and turn toward me. "Are you

kidding me?"

I laughed and stepped into the closet. "I'm not kidding you at all."

"Wow," she said. "Really, a week?"

I wrapped my arms around her, pulling her close and breathing her in. "I'm not joking. It's been a week."

"It feels like I've never left."

"You haven't left this house in nearly a week, Em." It was clearly messing with her mind and I didn't like that. Pressing a kiss to her neck, I held her tightly, never wanting to let her go. She meant everything to me. I couldn't get enough of her. I knew my friends felt this way, too.

"I'm so stressed." She rested her head back onto my shoulder. "Why do I feel this way?"

"It's your best friend and you know what is going to happen today. You're nervous. If Earl has agreed to bring Emily, then you need to know he's not hurt her in any way."

"Do we really need him on our side?" Emily asked.

"Why don't you wait to see Ashley to see what she thinks of everything happening? What if she likes belonging to Earl? You enjoy being ours."

"But that's different. I'm in love with you. Earl only wants her for what he can get and that's not good. Ashley deserves better. She wants to be a cook and write cookbooks, and make cooking shows, and do all that stuff. She's normal."

I slid my hand between the slit of her towel and cupped her pussy.

She gasped. "Vadik?"

"You need to relax. You're way too stressed, and panicking like this, it's not good for the soul."

She was wet for me. I slid my fingers across her

clit before moving down to plunge inside her.

In and out, I fucked her with my fingers, making her take me. With my other hand, I pulled on the towel and relished the sight of her naked body as it fell to the floor. Bruises covered her body and a fresh wave of anger erupted within me, but I didn't stop. Kissing her neck, I slid my tongue across her pulse as I began to fuck her cunt, getting her wetter for me.

She reached behind her, stroking my cock and I gritted my teeth, trying to gain control. I was so fucking hard.

Emily surprised me as she tore out of my hands, and then sank to her knees before me.

"You want to distract me, but I think it's exactly what I want to do with you."

I didn't fight her as she eased the top button of my pants open. She wanted to play and suck my dick, and I wasn't going to fight her. Reaching out, I stroked her face as she took my long length into her hand.

I grew harder with every passing second, and when her lips surrounded the tip of my cock, I was in heaven. I closed my eyes for a few seconds, counted to ten, and opened them. Control was what I needed. Her mouth was so perfect.

If she kept on teasing me, I wasn't going to last long.

Emily tongued the tip, sliding across the tiny hole before sucking me into her mouth. She took more of me this time until I hit the back of her throat. She gagged but it didn't last long as she pulled up. Then she released me to glide her tongue down the vein and all over my cock. I watched her, enjoying the way she loved my cock. With her tits out and her body on display. All I needed was a mirror and for her to spread those ass cheeks wide so I could watch.

Pulling away from her, I stepped out into her bedroom, and Emily crawled toward me. Her room had a full-length mirror and as I stood in front of it, she settled in front of me.

"Grab your ass and spread your cheeks wide," I said.

Her cheeks went a beautiful shade of red, but she did as I asked without a second's hesitation. I watched her do it and stared into the mirror. It wasn't perfect, but I saw her tight little asshole. Emily took me into her mouth and began to bob her head, sucking me hard and deep, but I couldn't tear my gaze away from her asshole. I wanted inside her, to claim her.

I once again pulled out of her mouth and this time, I reached for her, getting her to her feet and pushing her over the bed. Holding on to her hips, I was careful of all the bruises. I don't want to mark her perfect body. Finding her entrance, I slammed inside her pussy, hearing her cry out, the pleasure echoing around the room. I pounded inside her cunt, getting her nice and wet.

"Hold your ass open for me, princess," I said.

She hesitated for a few seconds, but I waited. I was a patient guy, and Emily needed this time to be distracted. I didn't care if Earl had arrived or not.

With her holding her ass open, I slicked up my fingers with my spit and applied it to her tight, puckered hole. She tensed up but didn't let go of her cheeks. I smiled as I worked a single finger inside her. She didn't stop me as I continued to fuck her pussy and spread her ass as I pushed another finger within her, using the two to begin stretching her ass. A gentleman may have given her time and a little more practice, but I'd never claimed to be a gentleman, and well, I wanted to take her asshole. I wanted to take all of her.

I eased out of her cunt and my length was covered with her arousal. I pushed the hard tip to her anus and her tension mounted. After I put a hand at the base of her back, I slowly worked past the tight ring of muscles and fed her asshole my dick. I watched her spread as I did. I was one of her masters, and her body was made to be fucked, to be pleasured.

Her anus was a lot tighter than her pussy, but I didn't care as I put my hands on her hips once again and held myself balls deep within her. She was still holding on to her cheeks and with my other hand, the one that hadn't played with her ass, I reached between her thighs and stroked her clit. I didn't intend to get her off, at least not yet, but to get her to a point where she started to fuck back against me. She'd be so perfect.

Teasing her clit, I felt the answering ripple as she squeezed me. The moment I suspected she was close to orgasm, I stopped touching her pussy and began to fuck her asshole. In and out, I was slow at first, allowing her to become accustomed to the feel of my large cock inside her.

"How does it feel?" I asked.

"Er, big … tight. A little too big."

"Do you want me to stop?" I didn't want to, but if she couldn't handle me or this, I'd wait patiently for her to be ready. There was a lot of fun to be had in waiting, in preparing as well.

"No. It feels good. I don't want you to stop."

I smiled. Our woman had a wicked side to her, and I wanted to explore that. I watched her, enraptured with how fucking sexy she was, taking all of my dick and moaning as she did. I stopped again to work her clit, drawing her closer to her orgasm, only to stop. She cursed me, telling me she hated me and to just let her come, but that would be giving in way too easily, and I wanted to make her wait for me, for this.

My orgasm was close but I wasn't going to come before her. Emily would be rewarded, and as I took her pussy and worked her harder than ever before, I immediately stroked her clit, bringing her to orgasm. Her pleasured cries filled the room as I stroked her. I didn't stop as she came, allowing her a few seconds to bask in her release, but when I couldn't take the tightness of her ass anymore, I started to fuck her, finding my release. I held myself deep within her and flooded her with my cum, closing my eyes.

Taking her asshole meant I hadn't helped my friends with getting her pregnant, but they'd understand. We all wanted to bind her to us. We hadn't come to the decision lightly, but we all knew what we wanted. I knew Caleb was scared of wanting her to be pregnant, but I knew Emily was a fighter. Not all babies were the same and what killed his mom wouldn't kill Emily. Even as I took her asshole now, I would help to knock her up. She was too tempting to deny.

"Wow," Emily said.

I leaned over her, kissing her neck and running my hands over her back. "I need to take you for a shower."

"A shower sounds good. I had no idea it could feel like that."

"It gets better. Wait until you're used to taking cock, you're going to crave it."

I kissed her, pulled out of her ass, and I had time to see some of my cum spilling from her cheeks before I picked her up in my arms and carried her through to the bathroom.

"Thank you for the distraction, Vadik, but I still don't have a clue what to wear."

****

Gael

The moment Earl Valentine walked into our home, I wanted to kill him. The only thing holding me back was seeing Emily and Ashley rush at each other and hug. I got that level of friendship, I did.

Caleb, River, Vadik, and I, we weren't huggers, but we were closer, always had been and always would be. I loved my brothers and I'd do anything for them. Earl had his own men at his back. He was a tall and well-built fucker. When I first heard about this bastard all those years ago, I'd expected some old dude with bald hair and a large beer gut. Not a clue why, but Earl, if we'd given him a chance, could have well and truly won our girl over, no doubt about it. As it was, he wasn't going to win anything, not from us, and certainly not our woman.

"I've missed you so much," Emily said, drawing my gaze.

"Missed you too." Ashley cupped her cheeks. "It doesn't look like you're happy." She shot a glare at us. "What did you do to her?"

"None of your business," Caleb said.

Emily waved her hand at us. "Don't mind them. I'll tell you all about it. Come on."

"What about dinner?" Earl asked.

I noticed Ashley tense up the instant asshole spoke. I couldn't see any visible bruises, and as Ashley glanced behind her, Earl was only interested in her.

"We've got business to attend to. If it would make you feel better, I'll have one of your men, as well as one of mine, escort them to a safe place where they can't run away together," Caleb said.

"I don't find this amusing."

"Well, seeing as we played our part in the deal

and you didn't, I'd say you've got a lot to be worried about. As it is, so long as our women wish us to play nice, nothing bad is going to happen. Ashley, do you want me to end this fucker now?"

In answer, Ashley looked behind her at him. She nibbled on her lip and finally, after a few minutes, she shook her head. "No, it's fine."

"I'll call our man," Caleb said, pulling his cell phone out.

"I'm already here," Drake said.

"Holy crap, Drake! As in crazy Drake?" Ashley asked.

Drake whistled and winked at her. "You sure look fine, sweetheart."

Emily rolled her eyes. "He doesn't even remember you."

"Sure do. New girl. You actually got this chick here all fired up in protecting you. I thought that was damn fine!" Drake whistled. "Where do you want them to catch up?"

"The library," Caleb said.

"Not a chance." This came from Earl.

We all turned toward him. I hadn't taken my attention from him, but now I looked at him.

"You think I don't know there's an exit in the library? Not happening. You're not stealing her away." Earl tensed up and I put my hand to my gun hidden beneath my jacket. I wanted any excuse for us to make this right with our woman, and if that meant popping him, then I was in a good enough mood to do it.

I watched him in case he decided to make any sudden moves.

"Our intention is not to steal her away."

"Good. She can go to your office then, Caleb. You're the one in control. We'll be the ones to go to the library." He moved toward Ashley, leaned down, and whispered something to her ear.

She pressed her lips into a firm line but stepped away from him.

That clearly displeased Earl.

It would all be easier if I just took him out. One glance at Caleb and he shook his head at me.

Fucker. It would do the entire world good to end this asshole.

But then, it would probably do more people good to end us. I kept my hand on my gun, but I didn't kill him. I considered this all progress.

Drake led the two women toward the office, while Caleb took the lead in walking us all the way to the library. I couldn't believe Ace was dead. Out of all the men, he'd caused us the least trouble during our takeover plan. He'd wanted death, and we'd kept him alive.

"You betrayed us and now you think you can come into our domain and bark orders?" Caleb asked.

"The only part of our arrangement I didn't keep was staying too close to you. You think I didn't know there would be consequences of staying close? That woman has all four of you by the balls. One snap of her fingers, and I'd be dead and Ashley would be free. I'm not that desperate and I'm certainly not an idiot."

"What about dealing with our fathers' prior arrangement to have Emily killed?" I asked, speaking up for the first time since he arrived. "What do you have to say about that?"

"I told you, I broke one part of our agreement. The other, I took care of. There wasn't a threat to Emily's life. All of the prior negotiations and bounty are over. I know how your fathers handled that mess, so I knew how to get rid of it."

This made me tense. I stared at Earl.

He wasn't a stupid man. "You knew how to erase it because you put it in place," I said.

Earl smiled. "Well, well, well, I had to wonder who would figure it out eventually. The fact it was you, I'm rather impressed."

"Cut the crap. You did this to start with. You gave them the ammo they needed to take Emily from us?" Caleb asked.

Earl sighed. "I need a drink." He stepped toward the drinks table, pouring himself a large shot of brandy. "Do you want one?"

In response, I glared.

"That's our booze, asshole," River said.

"I know." He took a sip, smacking his lips together. "Your fathers, they came to me with so many … options and concerns. They truly felt this girl, Emily, my intended, was a problem. Of course, she was supposed to be my sweet virgin, but we'll call that water under the bridge." He waved his hand across his face, then took another sip. "So good. They first wanted to kill Emily. To get one of their MC contacts. Make it look like a complete accident."

"Let me guess, you decided against that out of the goodness of your heart?"

He laughed. "I'm not that stupid. I'm a man who has built his empire from the ground up. I know you all have had this handed to you on a silver platter. It was so easy for you all, you merely took it. But for those of us who came from nothing, we had to bleed. You know nothing about me, and anything you do find out, well, it's not exactly the truth."

"Why don't you cut the crap and get to the part where we don't want to kill you? Right now, I'm feeling mighty ready to kill you," I said. My fingers were still wrapped around my gun, and it would be so much fun to just off him. To take his life. I wanted to more than anything else in the world. When I thought of Emily, I couldn't bring myself to do it. I loved her and I knew if there was anything he could do to keep her alive, I'd take it.

"Patience. Your fathers are not going to take a hit out tonight. They've lost one of their own. Congratulations for taking care of him. Ace, he'd been more for me killing Emily."

"You weren't down in that basement," River said. "You don't know what went on."

"I do know what they intended and I was the one who played out what would happen if your guys ever found out what they did. With their own personal sense of loss, they saw my reasoning was sound. They weren't exactly the sanest people around now, were they?" He finished off his shot. "So, I got them to make a deal. If you arrived, I would do as was negotiated. I'd put a hit out on Emily in the case of you following her. I was the one who set it up. Your fathers, they funded it. If you didn't arrive, they were going to handle Emily their own way."

"You think this is your helping your cause right now?" Caleb asked.

"Yes."

Vadik charged toward Earl and his guard drew his gun. I pulled out mine, aiming it at Earl. Caleb and River did the same.

The only one not carrying was Earl. He chuckled.

"Seven years. We've been in control for a lot longer than a couple of months. You had the power to bring us what we wanted. Why didn't you?" Vadik asked.

Exactly my thoughts.

"You think I'm just going to hand you what you

want? I knew you were all time bombs waiting to go off. Your fathers believed with Emily out of the way, they could control you. Week after week, month after month, I heard the damage you all were responsible for. At first, I had to make sure you had taken real power. Your fathers have a lot of friends, which I'm sure you're more than aware of. Then, I had to go see Emily for myself, to see that she was still alive, and that she'd even work to fit into my plans."

"Where does Ashley fit into all of this?" River asked.

"She's my reward."

"Do you hurt her?" Caleb asked.

"You've seen her for yourself. Does she look hurt?"

"I know there are a great deal of bruises that don't show up."

Earl snorted. "I don't hit my women."

"Don't treat us like fools. We know what you're capable of. The bodies that mount up from women you can't control," I said.

"Actually, that is business, and I have nothing to do with their deaths. To put your minds at rest, I can order Ashley in here to strip and you can see every single inch of her if you'd like, and while you're checking over my woman, I'll go to a room, and let's see what would happen if I was left alone with her for as long as you check mine."

Vadik charged forward and all of a sudden, Earl had a blade within his grip.

"I take my protection seriously. You think I won't protect what is mine? Ashley is mine. Try to take her from me, and I will make you all suffer in ways you've only ever imagined."

We stayed perfectly still.

Earl was a threat. One we didn't need, at least not now. I waited for Caleb to give the order. Killing Earl would be a mistake. We don't know the kind of power he held. If what he said was true, there was a great deal we didn't know. I hated those odds. Emily's life was too damn precious to all of us to waste it.

I waited.

Finally, Caleb cleared his throat. "I think it's time we get down to business and allow our women to catch up."

One. Two. Three. Four. Five.

Slowly, I made the first move in putting my gun away. Emily didn't need this tonight, and Ashley, well, we'd find a way to protect her, if she even needed it from us.

Chapter Fifteen

Emily

The moment we were far away from our men, I pulled Ashley into my arms. In the past seven years, Ashley had turned me into a hugger. I hadn't been one to show too much emotion.

Living with my dad and brother, as well as my driver, to survive, I'd learned to be cold, almost wooden in feeling and movement.

Ashely had not had the same troubles that I had. She felt so much and loved a great deal. She'd never been afraid to show it either. If we watched a sad movie, she'd sob her heart out and sniffle all the way through. When someone made her mad, she'd growl, scream, and even hit a pillow. I'd seen it. The person who had done the aggravation was never around when she let go.

"Are you okay? Did he hurt you? I'm so sorry for not being there. I've been trying to get you back. Are you okay?" I kept repeating the same questions over and over.

Ashley chuckled. "Stop, Em, stop."

I hugged her close, feeling so much guilt at what I nearly caused her.

"Hey, hey, it's okay, Em. I'm right here, and I'm fine."

I pulled away and started to lift the arms of the dress she wore. I didn't see any signs, but all of a sudden, she pulled away.

"You've got to stop." Ashley held her hands up.

"Does he hit you? Beat you? Rape you?"

"No!" Ashley yelled the word. "You've got to stop and calm down. Get your shit together or something."

"I'd say," Drake said.

I glared at him. "You get to be quiet. You don't have a single say in this."

"Thank God. You're acting like a crazy person. We don't know how long they're going to be, or how this is going to end. So shut up and let her speak."

I opened my mouth, closed it, and opened it again. I was a little taken aback by the sheer force of his words, but I couldn't deny it. I wasn't letting Ashley get a chance to speak and that was on me.

"I'm so sorry."

"Shut up, Emily," Drake said.

I placed a hand on my mouth and smiled up at my best friend. "I'm sorry."

She chuckled. "It's good to know that since I've been away you've found your voice."

"You'd be surprised." This from Drake again.

"I remember you being a lot more childish," Ashley said.

"I don't remember you at all," Drake said, winking at her. "But I'd like to get to know you."

"Stop it," I said, taking Ashley's hands and walking her all the way back to the sofa. Caleb's office wasn't exactly comfortable. Even the chairs left a lot to be desired in the comfort corner. "Tell me. Talk to me about everything. Is he good to you? Are you happy? Don't leave anything out."

Ashley sighed and looked toward Drake.

"I'll stand outside but I'm not going anywhere else."

"If you need us to take care of you, we will. I know my guys, they'll protect you."

"Emily, stop it. Okay. Yes, in the beginning, I was terrified. One moment I'd been asked to deal with a client who wanted to talk to me, and the next, I wake up on a boat or a yacht. I think it was more of a yacht. Anyway, Earl, he told me about the deal he made. Saving you, bringing you back here, and in return, he got me, or more importantly, my virginity."

"He has raped you." I stood up, ready to go and slice the prick up, but Ashley grabbed my hand and forced me to sit down.

"You need to stop. I'm still a virgin. We haven't had sex, okay?"

I frowned. "You haven't?"

"No."

"Why not?"

Ashley laughed. "Have you ever considered Earl might be a gentleman?"

This time I snorted. I couldn't help it.

"Emily!"

"What? I'm sorry. A gentleman doesn't make a deal to protect one woman, while he has every intention of taking her friend for sex."

"We haven't had sex and he has been so nice to me. I can't even begin to tell you how … he is. I think he's sweet."

"Honey, that's Stockholm syndrome talking."

"I thought that, but Emily, he's … he makes sure I'm happy. Yeah, I mean, at first, it wasn't easy and it has only been a couple of days, and he was a dick and he can be a pain in the ass, but, I … I think I kind of like him."

"Kind of like him?" This was a huge fucking deal. I mean, I don't even know how she could be thinking in terms of liking this asshole. He was only interested in getting a virgin.

Ashley shrugged. "I know it makes me sound like a pushover."

"You sound like you're protecting him."

"Maybe I am. He hasn't been bad to me, Em. I'm not an idiot. I know what he's all about. He's told me, but he's not the worst monster we've seen, is he?"

I paused.

"Your dad. He killed my mom and well, look at the mess he got us all into. I'd say he was our biggest problem."

I didn't want to admit that she was right, but she really was. My dad was a grade-A selfish asshole. If it wasn't for my men, we'd have both been dead, and the life we had together wouldn't have happened.

"I felt so guilty," I said. "They bargained your life for mine. I couldn't stand it."

Ashley cupped my cheek. "You know, in high school, I could see how devoted they were to you. I guess nothing ever changes."

I put my hand over hers. "I don't want to lose you."

"You're not going to lose me. I'm right here."

I couldn't help but pull her into me for another hug. I hated the way I felt. The guilt was still there. Ashley held me and I closed my eyes, hoping she was happy.

"Please tell me you're happy."

"Don't push it," Ashley said, laughing. "I know there are a lot of things in this life I was never going to get."

"The cooking show?" I asked.

"Just, I don't know. I think I pictured a life with a husband who adored me, and we'd have kids, a house, and a couple of dogs, cats as well. You know I'm crazy about animals."

I chuckled. With us both working, we hadn't been able to get a dog.

She sighed.

"Well, could Earl be the love of your life?"

Ashley shook her head. "I'd like to think there's a chance, you know, but he's made it abundantly clear he and I, we're not going to … he wants one thing from me. When he's ready, he'll get it, and take me until he's bored."

Now I felt sick, angered, and wanted to kill the bastard. I stood up, ready to do just that, but again, Ashley caught my wrist.

"How about we stop talking about my men and we talk about all of yours," Ashley said with a laugh.

"There are not that many."

"Has Drake joined your harem?"

"It's not a harem and ew, no, gross. Drake is … he's my guard, I think. And I believe we're also friends. I think so."

"You only think so?"

"You know how it is." I rubbed at my temple.

"I know how it was in high school. Clearly not a whole lot changed."

I stared at Ashley. Her smile. It didn't quite meet her eyes, and I hated myself for that. She was the optimist between us. The kind of woman to watch a romance film and wish she could find her Mr. Right. Earl wasn't it. If he only wanted her virginity, then I knew without a doubt she was only heading for heartbreak, and looking at her now, with my understanding of Ashley, she knew it too.

I took her hand. "You can always come back here. You got me."

Ashley squeezed my hands. "I know. I'm not afraid."

"You've got nothing to be afraid of," Earl said, startling us.

Caleb, Vadik, Gael, and River were by his side. I

hadn't even seen them come in.

I stood with Ashley, holding her hand.

"Dinner is served."

I tried to read them, to see if I had any idea what had gone down. Nothing.

Gritting my teeth, I stared at all of them.

"I'd like to talk to Earl," I said. The words spilled from my lips before I even realized I'd said them.

"Emily," Ashley said. I gave her hand a squeeze.

"Not happening," Caleb said.

Earl's brow was raised.

"He sought me out, after all. I'd like to talk to him. I think I can ask for that."

Ashley groaned. "You don't need to do the best friend routine."

"It's fine, Ashley," Earl said. "I understand."

My men looked like they wanted to dispute it, but I refused to budge. Ashley was my best friend. They hadn't looked out for her when I needed them to. Now it fell to me, and there was no way I was going to let her go to this monster without knowing firsthand what she was dealing with.

"No guards," I said. "You know this room has no exit. We'll come out."

"It doesn't stop him from killing you," Gael said with a growl.

"I won't kill her," Earl said.

"And we're supposed to believe you?" This from Gael again.

"Why don't you just accept that I know how to handle myself?" I asked. "I don't need any babysitters." I'd taken care of Gael back in high school. It was time for them to realize if they wanted me as theirs, they needed to stop treating me like a child.

"Fine," Caleb said. "We'll be right outside the

door."

Ashley passed Earl, and he grabbed her. I watched him. It wasn't a hard hold, but it was firm. I didn't like it. All it made me want to do was hurt him.

She stepped out.

The door closed and we were alone. Silence rang out.

I stared at him, in no rush to end this.

He made my skin crawl. I never liked him, and looking at him now, I still couldn't stand him.

"Is this where we have our little standoff, Emily?" he asked.

"I'm not having a standoff with you. I'm trying to get the correct words to say what I'm feeling, and if this was a standoff, I won."

He smiled. "Touché."

"Do you love Ashley?" I asked.

He laughed. "You're such a woman still. To fuck someone doesn't require emotion."

"I know." I glared at him. "You think I haven't known what men are like? You have only one interest in mind and it's popping a cherry then dumping her." I'd surprised him with my language. Years of being my father's punching bag, and knowing this world, I'd learned a thing or two. Women who spoke their mind, or were just plain blunt, well, it seemed to shock the men, and I'd do anything to have his focus on me than on my friend.

"You think that is all I want?"

"Ashley told me as much."

He smiled. "First, Emily, you think whatever we discuss right here and now, I'd even agree to or listen to? I can. I can pretend all I want to, but you've got no power here."

I stared at him for the longest time. In the back of

my mind, I knew my men are going crazy, wondering what I was doing. What the hell I was talking with this asshole about. I watched him, waiting for the moment he'd give something away for what he'd done to Ashley. I couldn't bear the thought of my friend being hurt by him.

"I think there is a lot more to your feelings about Ashley than you're letting on." I didn't look away but gave him my full attention.

"You let your imagination run wild."

"You're a businessman. My father organized for you to have my virginity for a hefty price. I also know you're a man who deals in women on a weekly basis. A virgin isn't so hard to find, yet you wait. You've probably had your share of virgins, and if not, the one you're waiting for is the person you intend to spend the rest of your life with. Women have biological clocks, but I also hear men have this need to gain an heir. To have someone to pass their legacy onto."

"You've been reading one too many books."

"And I also know that before you approach a possible target, you do your research. You're not a fool, Earl. You've been watching me and Ashley. Gaining as much knowledge as possible before even approaching us. I know Ashley. She's a different kind of woman than you're used to in these circles. She's strong, sweet, kind, loving. She has an innocent look on the world that you and I do not. It makes her alluring to us. Are you in love with her?"

Earl stared at me.

Time passed.

I waited.

I rarely had much patience, but it would seem when it came to my friend, I somehow found a great deal of it.

He opened his mouth, closed it, and walked to the door.

"If you hurt her, I'll kill you," I said.

Earl looked at me. "First, you'd have to catch me."

He exited the room and I was okay with that. I had a feeling I knew his answer, even if he didn't yet. Ashley, for now, was in good hands. He wouldn't hurt her. If he intended to, she'd have already lost her virginity.

****

Caleb

Dinner had been a tense affair.

Ashley and Emily had kept the conversation while me, my boys, and Earl had glared at one another.

Drake had also helped to carry the conversation along. They made no show of recognizing the tension. They were more than happy to talk. Now as I stood in my office, Earl and Ashley gone to a safe location of his own choice, I wasn't happy.

I threw the contents of my desk to the floor.

"Do you think that is going to help?" Emily asked.

I turned to see her already taking a seat on the sofa. She'd changed from the black cocktail dress into a rather revealing negligee. The curves of her breasts on full display and distracting me from my dark thoughts.

"You shouldn't come in here."

"Why? Because you're pissed?"

"You're not to be alone with that asshole."

"I agree," Gael said, entering my office.

River and Vadik were not too far behind him. Drake was nowhere to be seen. He did these little vanishing acts from time to time, and he always came back with information. There were moments I didn't think I could trust him. He'd been volatile during school and now he always seemed to be the perfect specimen of calm and control. I didn't buy it, but he had yet to give me any doubt as to his intentions.

"I didn't call for a family meeting," I said.

"No, you want to sulk all on your own. Not going to happen," Gael said.

Emily chuckled. "I don't see why you're sulking at all. This is a good thing."

I looked toward her with a question. "Vadik gave me the heads up," she said. "I know what you all talked about."

I glared at Vadik.

"Don't get angry at me. We promised we wouldn't keep her in the dark. Besides, she's part of this."

"Yes, I am," Emily said, sitting back.

"And how do you get that this is all a good thing?" I asked, pointing around the room.

She sighed. "You're in a mood because you have no reason to kill Earl. I'd say while he's helping us, he gets a free pass."

"Even though he's fucking your friend."

She shot me a scowl. "Anyway, the moment he does hurt my friend and all this crap is over, we can take him out. Not before then. We don't know what he's capable of."

"Emily, he's the one who made the deal to have you killed if we approached."

"And he's also the one who has made sure that didn't happen. Any attacks now come straight from your parents and you've also discovered there are men who want you all dead. I'd say that is a lot more important right now." Emily ran her fingers through her hair.

"You're being awfully reasonable about all of this," Gael said. "I thought the moment you saw Ashley, you'd want to cut his dick off."

"I do. I really do, but Ashley, she has always had a way that makes me calm and if she has the same impact on Earl, then I think we're all safe. I need you all to promise me you won't kill him. At least not yet."

"I'm getting whiplash," I said.

Emily rushed toward me. "I get that you're angry and you're stressed."

"Three fathers with a serious case of revenge are right now out there plotting our deaths. Not to mention they know how we all feel about you. I … I can't let anything happen to you."

She grabbed the back of my neck, pulled me down, and kissed me.

I couldn't resist grabbing her ass and holding her close. Letting her feel just how much I wanted her to be there.

Breaking from her lips, I trailed mine down to her neck, flicking across her pulse. Her moan filled the air and I groaned. In that instant, all I wanted was for her tight cunt to be on my dick, taking all of me. The desk was already clear and I spun her around, lifting her onto the desk and stepping between her spread legs.

She stared at me, and her hands moved across my chest, grabbing my shirt, and pulling it apart.

Buttons sprayed in all directions, and I didn't care. Sinking my fingers into her hair, I tugged her close and took her lips.

I sank my teeth into her lip as she rubbed my cock. Damn, I wanted her. I really did. Her negligee was flimsy against my strength and I had it torn from her body within a matter of seconds.

Her large tits ready for my mouth.

I loved the sight of her nipples, tightly puckered.

I didn't care that my friends were here. They knew how I felt. We all knew what each of us felt about this woman. At this moment, though, I didn't care what they saw or if they wanted to be in my place. All I cared about was getting my dick wet.

She pushed her hand inside my pants and grabbed my dick. I was already way ahead of her, unbuckling my belt, releasing my fly, and she pulled my cock free. I grunted as she ran her hand up and down the length, her thumb sliding across the peak. Pre-cum leaked from the tip and I gripped her neck, drawing her in, kissing her. With my other hand, I discovered she hadn't even bothered to wear any panties.

Feeling her slick heat, I fingered her pussy, running my fingers up and down her slit. Her clit was lovely and swollen. My need knew no bounds. Pushing her hands away from me, I bent down and took her cunt into my mouth. I slid my tongue inside her, feeling her begin to erupt against my tongue. I closed my eyes, enjoying her rocking against my tongue. I wanted her to take her pleasure, for her to be completely consumed by me.

Behind me, I heard my friends, and I had no doubt they all had their cocks in their hands, enjoying the show.

I ran my hands up her body, touching her tits. I gave them a squeeze, pressing them together. They looked so perfect. One day, I intended to slide my cock between those mounds and to use them until I came all over her chest with her mouth open to receive my cum.

There would be time for that because with Earl's help, I'd make sure she lived long enough for us all to enjoy the experience. All in good time. I came back to the present and all I was focused on right now was getting her off with my mouth. Staring up the length of her body, I watched as she closed her eyes, licked her lips, and then opened her eyes to watch me. Her gaze didn't just stay on me, though, it went behind me to my friends, and the look that crossed her eyes turned me on.

Her pussy was so freaking wet. She was aroused from seeing them, I just knew it.

Drawing my tongue up across her clit, I sucked her into my mouth, using my teeth to create just the right amount of pain that had her arching up. It was at the point where it was either too much or not enough, but I didn't care. All I wanted to do was make her come, and when she did, it was such a beautiful sight. She didn't hold back and I needed that. I craved every single part of her and all of her reactions. They were all mine to enjoy.

I wasn't done with her yet.

We hadn't worn condoms since she'd come back into our life, and I wasn't about to start now.

With my cock at her slit, I slowly began to fuck her wet lips. The tip brushing across her clit. It made her quiver with each touch. When I couldn't take another moment, I went to her entrance and began to fuck inside her. Going deeper than ever before. In and out, I took my time, building up the pace until I grabbed her hips, held on tight, and fucked her harder and faster than ever before, making her take all of me. Every single inch.

The desk didn't give way and I was so thankful for whoever's bright idea it was to have it nailed to the floor.

She took all that I gave her, wrapping her legs around me, and I felt the first stirrings of my orgasm.

I didn't hold back, though.

I gave it all to her, and as I came, her name spilled from my lips. She was everything I wanted and so much more. I could never be without her. Didn't want to and I knew as soon as our fathers were gone, we'd all finally be free.

Chapter Sixteen

Emily

Another new day.

Still stuck inside their home.

Well, I guessed it was my home now as well. It still seemed surreal to me to think of this place as my home, but this was how I was supposed to view it.

"Could you pass me the cumin?" Ashley asked.

I ran my gaze across the jars of spices.

After last night in the office, we'd all slept in the same bedroom, but when I woke, none of my men were to be seen, and I had Ashley's pretty face smiling at me. I loved her, but not enough for her to be that close, or to see me naked.

Back in London, I'd rarely slept naked because of Ashley bombarding into my room at any point, offering me up spoonfuls of food.

"I don't think we have cumin," I said, noting coriander, cardamon, cinnamon, and a few I couldn't even pronounce.

"Nope, it's here. I asked Earl to get it."

"And you don't think he screws up?"

"I know he doesn't screw up."

"He's a lot older than you."

Ashley laughed. "Is that what bothers you? The fact I don't want to run off and he's a much older guy?"

Before Ashley had taken over the kitchen, I'd given her the chance to run away. Drake would have helped, at least I think he would have. I wasn't sure. I still wasn't entirely sure if he was as loyal as he claimed. I just wasn't very good at believing people, and well, I guessed I needed to learn to have a little faith.

Ashley came over and instantly picked out a jar,

holding it up for me to see. "Cumin."

"Wow, you're like a kitchen warrior or something."

"I like to think of myself as more of a goddess." She offered me a smile, taking her teaspoon to measure out.

"What are you cooking, anyway?"

"Not a clue. Earl offered to buy me whatever I wanted and seeing as money isn't a question right now, I figure to have some fun and to just cook."

"It looks like a curry."

"It may be one."

I loved Ashley's curries, especially the coconut ones she did. Not too hot, but so much flavor. Just thinking about them back at her apartment made my mouth salivate.

"So, are you going to tell me all about Earl and your time with him?"

Ashley sighed. "So long as you tell me about you and your boys."

This made me pause. "What exactly would you like to know?"

She winked at me. "How about this, you ask a question, I ask a question. Deal? We've got to be open and honest with each other."

I wasn't so sure about this, but I agreed.

"You can go first," she said.

"What's Earl like?" I asked.

"He's … I don't know. There's nothing I can't have. Even when I suggest it, or make you know, wishes, he always finds a way of making it happen."

"How do you mean?"

"Nope. You don't get to ask that. One question at a time."

I groaned to which she giggled. "Are you

sleeping with all four men?"

I stared at her. "That makes me sound like a slut."

"Is that a yes or no?"

"Does that class as two questions?"

"You didn't answer the first one. Come on, no avoiding. That's cheating."

Running fingers through my hair, I nodded. "Yes, I'm sleeping with four men."

"Wow."

"Yeah, tell me about it." I honestly couldn't believe I was either. It sounded exhausting and yet here I was, more than capable of keeping up. "My turn."

"You already asked your next question."

"Right, but you didn't answer."

"Easy, I told Earl that I wanted to eat dinner while the sun set. To be out on the main boat thing. What's that called?" she asked. "You know where you can sit on the dock? Is it a dock?"

I shrugged. I didn't have any idea.

"Well, one night after I suggested that, I hadn't been allowed outside, but as the sun was setting, he brought me out, and as you can imagine, it was beautiful. We had some of the nicest food, and it felt like a real date."

"It sounds wonderful," I said, meaning every single word.

"It was. I think it may have been the first time I didn't see him as a monster." She shrugged. "My turn to question you."

"Go on. I'm all ears."

"Who is better in bed?"

"I cannot compare."

Ashley gave me a look.

"Is that sending me a question with those eyes?"

"No, and I'll give you that one for free. So,

they're all good in bed?"

"I've got no complaints. What is the sudden interest in my sex life?" I asked.

"Is that another question?"

Seeing as it was my turn, I nodded.

She stopped stirring, her teeth sinking into her lip. "It's nothing."

"Don't lie. Something is going on. I can smell it."

"That's the food."

"You're avoiding the question, Ash. Don't make me get that rule book you like to keep on you."

"It's not that bad."

"Come on, talk to me." I wanted to know. We'd gone seven years with the sex talk kept to a minimum. She'd gone on some dates, but not enough to make her want to have sex.

"I guess I know Earl wants to have sex with me. He's made it quite clear."

"And you want to?"

"I've always wanted to have sex, Emily. I'm not some paragon of virtue. I do want to know what it's like to be with a man. To see him completely drawn to me. No, not drawn, I want obsessed. You know, like they talk about in the books. The kind of men who only want one woman, and are desperate to be with her and would do anything to be with her."

"Wow," I said. "You've thought about it a lot."

She nodded. "There are times I catch him looking at me. I wonder if he sees me, or if he just sees the trophy he's got. I don't know." She rubbed at her temple. "My turn. Are you in love with them?"

"That is an easy one and the answer is yes. I love them. I love all four of them. Even when they drive me crazy, but I do."

Ashley laughed. "You know, I haven't seen you

this happy. The danger aside, your men are so good for you."

"It was never you, you know that, right?"

"Of course. You were heartbroken. Here try this." She held the spoon out toward me and I took a sip.

I winced at the sudden hit of heat and spice that burned the back of my throat. She saw my reaction, took a quick taste, and had one of her own.

"Easily fixed. Way too much heat, I need to balance that out. Some lime, methinks."

I drank some water in an attempt to rid my mouth of the taste. It wasn't her best. I knew Ashley, she'd get it just right.

Watching her work had always been fun. Her hands cutting, squeezing, sprinkling, stirring, tasting. She always looked off to the right when she assessed the flavor. Her lips pouting as she thought about it.

"It needs a touch more sweetness, and let's not forget the lime. Yum." She did that, another stir, and a taste. "Yep, I got it."

She offered me some and I hesitated. "Come on, Em, you know me."

"Yeah, and you could be punishing me."

"I've got nothing to punish you for. I'm happy. You're happy. As far as I can tell, we're all happy, and don't have a single reason to hate each other."

I took a sip and she was right, of course, she was.

"Are you cooking tonight?"

"Is that a question?" she asked, winking at me.

"I don't know, but who is next?"

She shrugged. "Ask away."

"Do you want Earl Valentine to be your first?"

She stopped and looked at me.

I didn't know what it was about my question that had her in such deep thought.

"Yes, Em. I do. I probably should hate him. He kidnapped me. Wasn't even polite about it. He's always blunt and to the point. He doesn't leave anything to chance and he's been honest with me from the start. Not a lot of guys are like that."

"True, but you can do better than him."

"Better than who?" Drake asked, coming into the kitchen. He wore some gym gear, and he'd been working out, even though he should have been on guard duty. He'd left us alone with one of Earl's men. I wasn't a big fan of being left alone with an asshole's minion, but at least I got to spend as much time with Ashley as I could.

"We're just talking about Earl."

"I can see that. It smells so damn good in here." He nudged Ashley out of the way and took the spoon from her, helping himself. He groaned. "How about you marry me?"

"No can do," she said. "I'm already taken."

"I think we should steal her," Drake said, looking toward me.

"I'm with you on that one."

"What are you two ladies doing for the rest of the day?" Drake asked, already ladling some of the curry sauce into a bowl. I watched as he grabbed some bread and began to dip it into the sauce and eat.

"I'm cooking. This kitchen is the bomb. I've missed cooking. Earl doesn't let me do this on the boat."

"You call it a boat?" Drake asked.

"It's what it is."

"It's a yacht, Ashley."

"Don't care. It is what it is. I don't have to remember every single little detail, do I?"

Drake shrugged. "When Earl's done with you, you can always come here and we'd put you up."

I watched the sadness Ashley quickly tried to

hide. Fuck! I had a horrible feeling she was already falling for Earl, and what was worse, he was only going to hurt her.

The bastard.

****

Vadik

I was tired, hungry, and wanted Emily.

She wasn't in the kitchen. We'd missed dinner, and after Ashley had left with Earl once again, she'd disappeared.

I checked her room, the garden, and as I came to the office, about to head on inside, the soft sounds of a piano playing drew my attention.

Drake had played for her last time, and he'd gone with Caleb to run an errand. Even though we had our fathers to deal with, work itself didn't stop moving.

We were still the bosses and had to make sure our work didn't implode on itself.

Emily sat at the piano, alone.

From the haunch of her shoulders, she looked sad. Stepping into the room, I was as quiet as possible, listening to her play.

Her fingers were light on the keys as she moved achingly slowly from one tune into another. When I sat down beside her, she didn't jolt or act startled.

"Sorry, I didn't mean to disturb you," she said.

"You didn't. You sound beautiful."

"I don't play all that much. I'm not good at it." She stopped playing, putting her hands between her thighs.

I didn't understand the sudden change in mood. Reaching between her thighs, I took one of her hands within my own.

"I'm here."

"I know."

"What is it you need? Tell me and I'll try to get it."

"It's nothing, Vadik. Really."

"Emily, I wasn't born yesterday. I know you're upset. Let me help you in any way I can."

She sighed. "I was thinking about Ashley."

"I know."

She turned toward me and smiled. "Is it that obvious?"

"You've become her protector. Of course, it is." I kissed her knuckles. "Do you have any reason to believe he's been a monster to her?"

"No. Quite the opposite, in fact. I know it makes me seem strange, but I just, can't we get rid of him?"

I looked down at her hands. "Yes, we can, Emily. You know that. We can take out whoever we want. It's what we do."

"There's a *but* there."

"There is always a *but*."

"Tell me why," she said.

"There are always consequences, Em. Like the men who took River when he was sixteen. They had to pay the price, but we also did. We had to fight and learn to take care of ourselves, even more than before. It swings both ways. Earl is not alone. He has contacts. He probably suspected before he arrived that we wanted to kill him. Anyone with any sense wouldn't enter Crude Hill without safeguards in place."

She turned toward me. "Ashley's falling for him. Her feelings, they're not … he's going to hurt her. I know he is and I can't think of a single fucking thing to do to stop it." She let go of my hands and covered her face.

I felt her pain but I had no way of relieving it.

I wrapped my hands around her.

She didn't cry. She growled and pulled away, getting to her feet. I couldn't help but admire the shape of her ass as she started to pace the length of the piano. I watched her. She hadn't put a bra on and the shirt clung to her body. Her nipples were nice and tight.

My cock instantly responded. I stood up, trying to relieve the pressure in my pants, but nothing would do as I watched her.

She suddenly turned toward me and when she flung herself into my arms, I held on tight. Running my hands to her ass.

"Make me stop thinking about them. About her."

I squeezed her ass cheeks, hearing her whimper as I applied a little more pressure than she was used to.

There was no a good surface in this room, but I didn't care. Removing my clothes, I broke the kiss long enough to get us both naked. The moment she was, I took a step back to admire her body. Sheer fucking perfection was what she was.

She sank to her knees before me. Her fingers wrapped around my dick, working the length up and down. Her tongue flicked over the tip leaking my pre-cum.

I ran my fingers through her hair, taking hold of the length in my fist and holding her tight.

She whimpered but covered the tip of my cock with her lips. With my grip, I forced her to take as much of me to the back of her throat. She gagged on my length and I relieved her, letting her breathe before sinking inside her again.

Saliva covered my entire shaft. She pulled off my cock and ran her tongue all over my dick, sliding down the vein and coming back to suck me again.

I pumped within her mouth, feeling the start of

my orgasm, but I didn't want to come inside her mouth. Pushing her away from me, I got to my knees. With my grip tight on her body, I moved her to exactly where I wanted her to go. Holding her in place, I found her entrance and fucked her tight and fast. She moaned my name and I loved the sound as it echoed around the room.

In and out.

I spread the cheeks of her ass to see my cock riding her cunt. So pretty. So perfect.

All mine.

All of ours.

I couldn't explain how I felt with her or my friends. If it was anyone else, I couldn't share her. Wouldn't want to. Gael, River, and Vadik, they were more. They were everything. They were our life. Every single part of it, and I didn't want to lose them or Emily. The life we had planned to spend together was the life I'd always wanted.

I held myself perfectly still at the hilt within her, feeling her pussy ripple on my length.

Reaching between her spread thighs, I started to stroke her swollen clit, bringing her closer to orgasm. I had no interest in stopping, but I needed her to come first.

The moment she did, I worked her pussy until she was screaming my name. I loved the sounds on her lips.

Only when I couldn't stand to wait anymore did I grab her hips and fuck her until I came, releasing wave upon wave of release into her body.

Afterward, I collapsed on top of her. Her knees had already given out. I kissed her neck and wrapped my arms around her.

"Did I ever mention that I missed you?"

She giggled. "I think I'm getting the idea."

"I thought about you every single day. Not a moment went by when we all didn't regret letting you go," I said.

"I felt the same way. All four of you. I'd dream of you and I'd think what life would have been like if only we'd gotten the chance to be."

I pulled out of her tight pussy and she turned to look at me. I brushed a stray curl off her forehead and dropped a kiss to her lips.

"There is something I want to show you."

Getting to my feet, I offered her my shirt as I pulled up my jeans. I'd already snatched her used clothing from the floor so she couldn't change into it.

I took her hand and she didn't fight me, which I considered a bonus. After walking out of the room, we headed upstairs. I went to my room, and more specifically, the closet that I had removed all my clothes from.

I had drawers, and I hung my suits when I needed to wear them on my bathroom wall. Switching on the closet light, I stepped back and allowed Emily to see what I'd created.

She gasped, putting a hand to her mouth. "Vadik?"

"I know this is stalker territory and I am sorry about that. Actually, no, I'm not sorry. I … this kept me sane. Or as sane as was possible." Every time I missed her, I drew. She was my muse. The very object of my obsession and I had channeled that need into my art.

"They're beautiful."

"You are beautiful," I said, touching her shoulder. "You're not afraid?"

She shook her head. "You know, Ashley talked today about having a guy who is so completely devoted to her. How can this scare me when it's exactly what I want as well? Only I've been lucky because I've been able to find four guys who want me, not just one." She turned toward me and there were tears in her eyes. "I wouldn't go around showing everyone this. They might get the wrong impression, but wow, Vadik."

"You're the love of my life, Em. I had to have a little piece of you in some way."

I thought I would've scared her with this, but instead, it had done the opposite. She threw herself into my arms and I lifted her, carrying her through to my bed. This was my dream. To have her in my arms, to make love to her, and every chance I got, to make her mine.

My dream had finally come true.

Chapter Seventeen

Emily

They had locked me in my fucking bedroom.

I tried the door for a second time and stepped back, even angrier than before. Caleb had come marching in the door because there had been a sighting of their fathers with a small army. To save me or to keep me safe, they'd locked me in my bedroom like I was some spoiled child.

I slammed my hand against the wood. Drake was nowhere to be seen. There was a guard outside my door, who'd been told to ignore all of my requests.

Annoyed, I used my foot and tried to kick it in.

Nothing.

"Fucking assholes." I was so pissed. "If you think you are going to get to sleep with me, you're so wrong. Do you hear me? I don't care who hears. You're not coming near me. none of you are."

Again, I slammed my hand against the door.

Stepping back, I took a deep breath.

Sitting on the end of my bed, I ran my hands down my thighs. They wanted to play at protectors, that was fine, but I should get the choice of how I stay safe, and being locked in my bedroom wasn't going to cut it.

The house was already driving me crazy.

I stretched my neck to the left and the right. Taking a deep breath, I turned toward the doors overlooking the garden.

"Don't do it, Emily. Don't do it." I spoke the words aloud even as I walked toward the door. I put my hand to the cold glass.

I'd been too busy fighting with Caleb to even give these doors a thought. Had he?

I didn't know.

Licking my lips, I tested the handle and laughed, quickly slapping my hand over my mouth to keep quiet. I looked toward the door, expecting the guard to come in at any moment to take all of this away from me.

He didn't.

Opening the door, I stepped out onto the balcony. It had started to get cold and the wind took me by surprise. The drop wasn't too far. If I was careful and lowered myself down, I'd make it.

But, just in case, I rushed back into the bedroom, stripped the bed down, and grabbed the sheet. I tied it around one of the balcony's posts. I was being completely irrational, but Caleb had taken this one step too far.

I got it. They were all worried about me. I accepted that, but I was not going to be a prisoner in that house anymore.

I'd tasted freedom and I wanted it back. There were many things I could live with. Their reputation, what they did to stay in control. I could handle all of it, but being a prisoner, not happening. Not anymore.

Climbing over the balcony, I grabbed the sheet, knowing if I fell wrong, I was so going to suffer for it.

Why was I doing this?

I was afraid of heights at the best of times.

Taking a deep breath, I tried to shimmy down, but I felt the blanket move. As I looked up, sure enough, the knot wasn't strong enough.

Before I even had time to move, it was untied and I fell down, hitting the ground beneath me. I rolled over with a groan, wanting to go back five minutes to remind myself I wasn't some kind of wall-scaling expert. I was a human.

I didn't have much time to lick my wounds or

revel in the pain. Voices came closer and I got to my feet, moving into the shadows. Guards passed and I just hoped they wouldn't catch sight of the blanket.

They didn't show any signs of seeing me.

When they were out of earshot, I moved out of the shadows, coming away from the wall, and I smiled. So far, so good.

Now, all I had to do was make a run for it. I'd show them. I'd show all of them.

I made it around to the main drive, seeing four cars parked in the driveway.

Rather than attempt to run on foot, I tried each door. Getting to the last one, I slid into the driver's seat and looked for the keys. When I found them, I smiled.

After clapping my hands together, I slid them into the ignition just in time for the door to open.

I stopped and turned to see Drake in the passenger seat.

"Planning a little escape?"

I turned the ignition over and he put the car into reverse.

I wasn't a very good driver. Ashley was the one who could drive.

"Emily, what the fuck?"

"I don't give a shit what Caleb and the others say. I am in control of my own life."

He slammed the door closed but I didn't care. I was too far gone on my own anger to give a shit about what he had to say or do. "I will not be ordered around like a child."

"Even though you're behaving like one."

"Fucking asshole. Do you think I'm in the mood to be told what I am or not reacting like? Huh?" I pressed my foot on the gas. "I suggest you make those gates fucking open, Drake. I'm not going to stop."

"Turn the car around."

"No."

"Emily, this is stupid."

"Being forced into a bedroom is stupid. This is one last-ditch attempt at freedom, and guess what, buster, I'm taking it." I burst out laughing, feeling like a crazy person had taken over, and maybe they had.

I wasn't going to be forced into my bedroom to be told what to do. My dad was long gone.

Caleb certainly wasn't going to get away with acting like it.

The gates started to open, but rather than slow down, since they weren't open wide enough, I scratched the car on the way out, taking a sudden spin to avoid a couple more parked cars.

Again, I wasn't a very good driver. I often took public transport for safety reasons.

Putting the car into gear, I lightly pushed my foot on the gas and we started moving.

"Do you want me to take over?" Drake asked.

"No."

"How did you get out of your bedroom?"

"Why were you back? I thought you were out running errands."

"I did all of them and I came back. I happened to notice you nearly fall and break your neck. What the fuck were you thinking?"

I glance over at him. "You were in the garden?"

"Of course."

"Then why ask me if you'd already seen what I was doing?" I asked.

"Wanted to see if you'd lie to me."

"Are you for real right now?"

"What? You're the one who actually tried to scale out of a window with a badly tied bedsheet. What the fuck were you thinking?"

"I think it's clear I wasn't exactly thinking anything now, was I?" I asked with a growl.

"How about I drive?"

"Not a chance."

"Em, you can't do this."

"I can do whatever the hell I want, and if that means I put my life at risk, then so be it." I pressed my foot to the floor and I knew, of course I knew I was being completely ridiculous. The only place I'd wanted to be for the past seven years was with those four impossible, irritating, annoying men. They were the Monsters through and through, but they were all mine. I knew it now more than ever.

There were times I had no idea how it was going to work. Four men, one girl. Would they get bored of me? It was a freaking possibility. A scary one, in fact, and it terrified me that I would never be enough for them, or they would realize how inconvenient it was to have one woman, and they'd trade me in. Not to mention how they would feel if I was to actually become pregnant. Would they want me then? Could we even survive with kids? I'd seen firsthand what it was like to be a kid in this world. To have parents who were monsters. Just the thought of my men hurting our child, it wouldn't happen. They were Monsters, but not like their parents, not when it came to their own flesh and blood.

All of these thoughts were not exactly good to have as I was traveling haphazardly down a street that I specifically recalled led to the Crude Hill High School. It would only be fitting if I actually ended up driving this death trap into the school. It was the first place where all of my troubles began. Not that I could call falling in love with Gael trouble, but if I hadn't reacted when I did, he would've been dead now, and me, well, I'd be at Earl

Valentine's mercy.

I couldn't help but wonder, though, if he wasn't such a bad guy. During the day I'd spent with Ashley, she didn't show any signs of emotional or physical distress. She may think I'd developed a crush on her with how many times I kept on staring at her. I loved her as a friend, but I was worried about her. Earl wasn't a good guy, but maybe, like with my Monsters, he was good for her. Maybe he loved her and that was what made him a good guy. Again, I didn't really know. I was hoping. That was what I was doing. I couldn't help but hope she was happy. That she was in the best place possible with Earl and he'd give her a wonderful life. If not, then I would have no choice but to kill him.

Ashley deserved the best life. She'd given me seven years, and I hadn't exactly been the nicest person to live with. I'd sobbed, and when she'd found positivity, I hadn't.

Running my hands down my face, I wanted to do nothing more than sob, but instead, I controlled myself. Taking long deep breaths, I slowly brought the car to a stop, up to the curb on the school grounds.

I hadn't even bothered with the seatbelt.

"Emily?"

I fumbled with the car door handle and finally got it open. Spilling out of the car, I wasn't exactly graceful, but I got there.

At first, I stared at the ground. The scent of wet grass was heavy in the air. Slowly, I drew my gaze up to stare at the school.

In the dark, it looked haunted.

With my arms folded, I just stared. Drake got out of the car and joined me. "You okay?"

"I'm fine." I whispered the words, not wanting to make too much of a sound. It could wake the dead.

Licking my lips, I stepped away and then decided to take a step toward the imposing building.

"I hated this place," I said.

"I think we can all safely say we hated this place."

"Really? Even you?" I asked.

He smiled. "I ... this was not just a place for kids of monsters, Em. This was a place where assholes like my father dumped the kids they didn't want to own up to."

"You've got a lot of issues when it comes to your father."

"He's the one who gave me a lot of crap. He hated me and I guess I loved him, but that quickly turned to hate." He blew out a breath. "Damn, you know I pass this place so often and I don't even take the time to look at it."

I forced a laugh. "I've done nothing but think about this place. I hated this place, but it was by far better than my home life."

"How come?"

For a second, I was confused, because I figured he knew about my past but then it wasn't like he was cushy with the Monsters back then.

"My dad, he'd beat me and put me through virginity checks. My driver hated me and to make my life worse, he'd lie and say guys were sniffing around me, or he'd be this arrogant prick, and he'd get to watch me being punished."

"Tell me he's dead?"

"Oh, he's dead all right. It turns out my father had been plotting to oust the Monsters. He got caught. My brother, mother, all of my family, and the driver, they were all killed."

"You were spared."

"Yep. I was sent to England with Ashley. Her mother was having an affair with my father."

Drake laughed. "And you guys are friends?"

"Her mother was in the firing line as well, Drake. Me and Ashley, we're the only two who made it. We were supposed to die that night all of those years ago. It's only because of their sons that we're still alive."

"Well, that answers the question about why you're so worried and so loyal to your friend."

"She's worth it. She has been there for me every single step of the way." I sighed. "I'm sure you know all about loyalty."

"Here we go. You still think I'm a traitor?"

"I don't know what to think when it comes to you. But I don't trust you." I unfolded my arms and screamed at Drake just as a man clocked him around the back of the head with a wooden baseball bat.

Drake didn't even have time to move. He fell, hitting the ground with a thud. I stared into the eyes of Marshall Keller.

"I knew we should have killed you when we had the chance."

The rage in his voice took my breath away. Rather than try to understand why he was so pissed, I turned on my heel and started running.

It was a big mistake. Within seconds, he was on top of me, shoving me to the ground. I let out a scream, hating that I was on my front. He grabbed my hair, jerking my head up, and I whimpered at the pain.

"I'm going to take every single ounce of pleasure in killing you." He licked my cheek, making me gag. Rather than fight, I acted as though I'd fainted. Literally slumped to the ground. Women did that all the time in movies because of fear, right? This was what I was doing. I was afraid. My body was nothing more than a dead weight, but it did the trick. I noticed when he wasn't so heavy on top of me, and he fumbled for something. I hoped it wasn't his damn belt. I reacted quickly, suddenly pushing my weight and spinning over.

The action jerked him away from me, but it didn't get the job done.

We were a tangle of limbs, and he managed to get his hands wrapped around my neck, cutting off my air supply.

At first, I gripped his hands, but he was close enough to me that I was able to clock him around the face. I jabbed at him, once, twice, and then I tried to poke him in the eye. My vision was slowly fading. I kept on fighting, trying to get him to get off me.

I was going to die on the school grounds, and fear lodged inside me. I didn't want to die. There was a life with my men. I hoped they all knew that I loved them so damn much. Even though I was pissed and tried my escape, I loved them all.

"Fucker!" Drake was there, thrusting a knife into Marshall Keller's throat, and I didn't have time to move away as blood spilled from the wound and a dead Marshall fell on top of me.

I breathed in hard and deep.

Drake helped me to push his body off.

With a hand at my throat, I took deep breaths, but it hurt to do so.

"They're coming, Em. I promise, they're coming." He pulled me into his arms, holding me.

His arms were the wrong ones. I only wanted my men.

****

River

I was never going to forget the way Emily looked

when we found her last night. We called our doctor to run some tests on her.

Marshall hadn't crushed her throat, but it had been a close call. Way too fucking close for my comfort. I didn't like it and as I sat in her bedroom now, watching her sleep, I thought about how close we'd come to losing her.

Drake also hadn't left.

"I thought you said you didn't have any feelings for her?" I asked, not taking my eyes away from my woman, not for a second.

"I don't."

"Then why the fuck are you still here?"

There was a brief silence and I chanced a look toward him.

"I fucked up last night. Emily could have died because of me. I didn't want that to happen, ever. There is no way that man should have gotten the best of me and yet he did."

"He hit you over the head with a baseball bat," Emily said.

I looked toward her.

Her voice sounded raw. Considering the bruises all around her neck, the fact she could talk was a bonus.

I got to my feet, leaning over her, kissing her head.

"I don't think your dads approve of me as yours," she said.

I laughed. "Don't joke around."

"Kind of have to. It's funny if you think about it. Your parents can't stand me. Isn't it every girl's dream?" she asked.

Shaking my head at her, I sat down. She looked at Drake. "Thank you."

"I'm sorry, Em."

"You didn't know he was there." She sighed. "Thank you for not being completely knocked out for longer."

I didn't care about Drake or his feelings right now. The only person I cared about was this woman right here, in this bed.

"Will you go and let the others know she's awake?" I asked.

Drake left seconds later.

"He feels guilty," she said.

"Good, he should."

"He didn't know."

"Em, you nearly died. He told us what happened. Marshall nearly killed you."

"But, and this is a big but, he didn't. I'm still here."

"In pain."

"I'm used to the pain."

I got up and kissed her head again. I was about to sit down, but she grabbed my shirt and pulled me to the bed. "Don't leave. Sit with me. I love you, and I don't want you to leave me."

I smiled. I couldn't help it. I still had my shoes on, but I didn't bother to remove them. Instead, I held her close, wrapping my arms around her.

"I don't want anything to ever happen to you," I said.

"Nothing is. I think I'm proving to be a little invincible."

"Em, you came close to being strangled."

She sighed. "I know. Marshall had it in for me. I guess that means two down, right?"

"Yes, and we have a feeling the other two are not going to be far behind."

"What do you mean?"

I didn't get a chance to answer her question as Vadik, Caleb, and Gael spilled into the room, all of them looking relieved to see her awake. She'd been awake when we'd gotten to her, but since the doctor looked her over, she'd been out for the count. I understood their worry. I was terrified when Drake called us. We could have lost her today.

"Are you okay?" Gael asked, coming to the bed.

"I'm fine."

"You don't sound fine," Vadik said.

"Well, I had a man trying to kill me. Forgive me if I don't look my best."

We all chuckled, but we all didn't see the humor. Our dads were the worst kind of men. Well, not the worst, but they knew our weakness. Emily. We didn't want to live without her.

Stroking her hair, I pressed my face against her head and breathed her in.

"Are you going to tell me why you think the others are suddenly going to come out of the woodwork? Marshall and Ace are now dead."

"Yes, which leaves Dean and Daniel," Gael said.

"Your dad and yours," Emily said, looking toward Caleb.

"Yep."

Emily sighed. "You're making me work for answers here, and I'm the victim. Can't you at least, I don't know, help me out?"

"Earl put out a call, a reward if you will," Caleb said, perching on the edge of the bed. "Anyone working for your fathers will be given a reward to come clean and for information. We've had five people within two hours of him putting out the reward."

"I thought you were hunting them down?" Emily asked.

I held her a little tighter.

"Earl wants to leave. He wants to take Ashley and have this business over with. He's not going with stealth, but speed."

Emily tensed in my arms. "But?"

"Emily," Caleb said. "If this works, then it means Earl kept his part of the bargain."

"What about Ashley?"

"She's happy," Caleb said. "I've checked. Drake has been gathering information and Ashley is being treated like a queen. She isn't in any danger."

Tears filled her eyes and I wanted to do whatever was necessary to take them away.

"I want to talk to Ashley. Do you think you can arrange that?" Emily asked.

Caleb nodded. "Of course. We still have two problems, and he promised he wouldn't go anywhere else until the matter is resolved."

"I can't believe you guys are working together over this," Emily said.

"Neither can we. Don't forget, we're still in shock as well. He wanted *your* virginity."

Emily laughed. "I know. His obsession for a virgin is scary. It makes me wonder if he's even any good in bed."

We all tensed up and Emily shook her head. "I don't mean I'm going to try him out. Wow, what kind of woman do you think I am? I've already got four men. I worry about Ashley." She dropped her gaze, wiping beneath her eyes before lifting up to look at me. "And today, when Marshall was strangling me, all I wanted was to get back to all of you. I don't want to live my life without you guys in it. I love you more than anything else in the world." She sniffled.

She sat up, pulling away from me. Then she

turned toward me, cupping my cheek and kissing me. I sank my fingers into her hair, holding her close, wanting her and only her. She pulled away, kissing Gael with the exact same passion, before going to Vadik, finally, Caleb. She showed us her feelings with a single kiss.

I smiled.

"I love you all so much. I don't want to ever be anywhere than where I am right now."

"Good, because we were never going to let you leave," Caleb said. He stroked her face and Emily sat back.

"However, we are going to need some ground rules," she said.

We all groaned.

"You were only buttering us up and letting us think you'd play nice."

She laughed. "I think it will work for all of us. I don't want you guys to push me out. I get that I'm a woman, and I'm not part of your little crew. I do, but don't manhandle me to the bedroom. It pisses me off. I can protect you as much as you can protect me. I've proven myself to you time and time again." She glared at Caleb. "Yes, I'm talking to you. No more marching me into a bedroom because you think it's the best place for me. It's offensive and rude."

"I will only ever act in a way to protect you."

"Yeah, I've got a feeling you're going to be my biggest rule-breaker," she said.

I couldn't help but laugh. Even though her voice was croaky and less than twenty-four hours ago someone had tried to kill her, she was back to being our woman.

"Is that your only rule?" Gael asked. "I don't like sticking to a whole lot of them. I enjoy breaking them."

"You've all got to promise me you'll kiss me every single chance you get, love me more and harder each day. Never get jealous. To love each other, and to never fight."

"We can't promise you we won't ever fight," Vadik said. "It's in our blood."

"Well…" She stopped as though to think for a few seconds. "Then you have to agree not to do any permanent damage. I don't want any of you to be in pain or hurting. We're a family now, right? We're all together and this means we're all we've got for the rest of our lives."

I took a deep breath and waited for the others to respond.

"I agree," Gael said. "It's not like any of those are going to be hard."

One by one, we all agreed to her terms.

Emily came toward me, straddling my waist. "Your throat," I warned.

"I don't care. I don't want to miss a single chance with all of you." She took possession of my lips. "Unless, of course, you're not up to the job?"

I gripped her ass tightly. "Emily, you could never be a fucking job." I pulled her down and slammed my lips down on hers, kissing her harder than before.

Chapter Eighteen

Gael

My cock was rock-hard.

We hadn't discussed us being present when she was fucked by one or more of us. I'd seen her with Caleb, and I'd been the first one to freely get my cock out and to watch that pretty show.

Like now, fuck, she looked so beautiful. Those perfectly large tits with tight nipples, they were a dream.

River, he licked and sucked at those buds, and I already had my dick in my hand. I'd changed from the tight confines of the trousers into a pair of sweats. Working my cock up and down, I rubbed my pre-cum into the length and groaned. River laid Emily down on the bed and took care of her panties, tearing them from her body.

Her neck was badly bruised. I had stayed to see Marshall's body get taken care of. Dean and Daniel, they were close, I could sense it.

My dad, I'd gotten used to the kind of pain he caused, and I knew he would gladly take Emily away from me. He'd see pleasure in my pain. When he finally came out into the open, I wanted to be the one to finally kill him. I'd wanted to a couple of years ago.

Caleb's plan to hurt them in that way hadn't been mine. He'd been the one to decide their fates. I knew I should have fought harder, but I'd wanted them to suffer. Even though we'd taken over from the empire, their fear still ruled. Slowly, we'd obliterated all of their traces, at least, we thought we had, but we'd been mistaken.

Pushing those thoughts to the back of my mind, I forced myself to only think of the now. Our woman, spread on the bed, within touching distance with River, who had his face pressed into her pussy.

His mouth made her scream and whimper. My mouth watered for a taste of her. I knew how good she was, and as she came, it was the most beautiful sight. Her chest flush, her nipples tight. Every single part of her, perfection. I wanted her so much, but I knew I was going to have to wait my turn.

River was rock-hard, and he lifted Emily so she straddled his waist. I moved from the bed to get a better angle. He spread her cheeks while she grabbed his cock, and slowly, she started to sink onto him. This was better than I could have imagined, and she took him so prettily. River didn't let go of her ass but used it to guide her up and down his length.

At first, he started to go fast, to take her deeper. She whimpered, moaned his name, and he sped up, forcing her down onto him as he thrust up. Emily wrapped her arms around his neck, holding as he fucked her. I worked my cock, and I knew Caleb and Vadik were doing the same. All of us knowing we wanted where River was right now, but waiting our turn.

When River finally came, his pleasure filled the room and I saw how tightly he held her. There would be bruises on her hips from his control.

"Thank you," River said.

She kissed him deeply, and much to my surprise, climbed off him. She turned toward us, her gaze going to all of us. I didn't have time to look elsewhere as she came toward me. Emily was full of surprises tonight as she slowly sank to her knees before me. She pulled my sweatpants down so they fell to my ankles and then her mouth was over my cock.

I let go of my shaft, sinking my fingers into her hair and feeling her tight lips swallow me up. I thrust inside her, hitting the back of her throat, only for her to pull away and then bob back in.

She worked me over and over, and I was so close. I wanted to last for her, but with how perfect her mouth was, I didn't have any control. I came, spilling between her lips and sliding down her throat. She let out a moan as she swallowed every last drop.

Fuck!

Perfection.

Sheer fucking perfection. That was what she was.

I loved her more than anything in the world. Dean's and Daniel's days were numbered. I didn't want her to go on living afraid. We had a life to lead. Seven long years to catch up on. It was time for us to start living them and not staying in the past.

****

Vadik

I had a feeling I knew what Emily was going through. She almost died tonight and it scared her. As I watched her suck Gael, I understood what she meant. When Drake called us and told us what had happened, I'd been so fucking scared. I hadn't agreed with Caleb putting her in her room like a scolded child, but he meant well. Fear made us all do shitty things.

We'd proven time and again we couldn't lose her.

We were the ones who had fucked up when it came to Emily. We put her life in danger rather than taking care of our dads when we had the chance.

Two were left.

Some men might have felt a slight bit of remorse at their parents dying. Not me. I felt nothing. Absolutely nothing.

Marshall Keller had taken the only thing that had any meaning to me. He'd put me through hell, and for that, I could never forgive him. Seeing his dead body tonight had filled me with pleasure to know he was dead and he could never hurt me or my loved ones again.

I heard Gael's moan of pleasure, and Emily got to her feet, moving toward me. The bruises around her neck angered me. The smile she gave me, though, that was worth everything in the world.

She came toward me, and I didn't care that she had Gael's cum on her tongue. I pulled her close and kissed her. Sliding my hand down to her ass, I lifted her and placed her on the edge of the bed. Her hands were already on my trousers, opening up the belt, then sliding down the zipper. I'd been touching myself but through my pants. I wanted to show some kind of control, but it had been for nothing.

As if I could ever really have any kind of control with this woman.

The instant she pulled my cock out of my pants, I felt so much fucking relief it was unreal.

I closed my eyes, basking in the few seconds of pleasure, and then it was torture as she worked up and down my cock.

Swatting her hand out of the way, I moved to her cream-filled pussy.

River's cum was already spilling down her thighs, and there was no jealousy. She was ours. She belonged to each of us.

Finding her entrance, I pushed inside, feeling her sweet walls come around me.

She'd been fucked with River's cock, and she was still tight, but she was even wetter. River had gotten her prepared to take us. Gael had wasted his chance by having her mouth, but damn, she did have a pretty set of lips. Taking possession of her mouth again, I kissed her deeply as I fucked her.

"I love you," she said.

I'd heard her say the words to each of the men. I wasn't sure if they heard her confession and as I rode her pussy, I didn't care. All I cared about was having her, taking her, loving her, fucking her.

What I wanted more than anything else was to fill her cunt with a baby. I craved control of her in every single way that counted.

I wasn't trying to control her with getting her pregnant under the belief she'd never leave. No, what I wanted was to see her heavily pregnant with our baby. To get started on the next generation of Monsters.

I felt the first stirrings of my orgasm and I pulled back enough to begin teasing her pussy. I ran my fingers over her clit, feeling the answering pulse around my dick. She moaned my name and I continued to tease her, loving the way she closed her eyes and arched up against me.

She was so close, but I wanted to feel her come on my cock.

Thrusting into her, I took my time, and after a few strokes of her clit and my cock within her, she came. With how good it felt, it set off my own orgasm. I continued to stroke her clit, joining her in release as I came hard, flooding her cunt with my arousal.

I closed my eyes, seeing stars and knowing in my heart of hearts, we were going to make it.

****

Caleb

I felt responsible for the bruises around her neck. The truth was, when it came to Emily, I had to protect her. I'd lived without her for seven years and that had been a nightmare. Living with her dead couldn't happen. I wasn't my dad. There was no future for any of us. No heir to bring into this world if we didn't have Emily.

I'd fucked up, I knew that.

Emily wasn't a woman to protect. She didn't want to be pushed into a corner, nor did she like being treated as if she'd break.

Vadik stepped away from her and I moved to her, stepping between her thighs. She was still coming down from her orgasm.

"I'm sorry," I said.

She offered me a smile. "Then don't do it again. Promise me."

"I promise I won't dump you in your room, but I will do whatever I can to protect you."

"Caleb!"

"I accept that you're going to be pissed. I do. I love you more than anything else in the world. You know that." I stroked her cheek. "I didn't know it was possible to even feel this way, but like always, you take me by surprise."

"I'm not angry at you anymore. Stop spoiling this and fuck me already." She winked at me and sat up, but I pushed her down to the bed.

If she wanted to be fucked, then I was more than happy to oblige.

I flipped her over so she went to her knees. I admired the curves of her ass, spreading the cheeks wide. I'd been planning to take her ass, but one look at that juicy pussy, and I knew where I wanted to go.

After sliding my trousers down, I worked my length, already feeling like a randy teenager, ready to spill into her waiting cunt.

Pressing my tip to her entrance, I slowly slid in deep. I didn't care about River or Vadik taking their pleasure within her. All of our cum deep within her was where it was supposed to be.

Her pussy was still having little aftershocks of

pleasure and I closed my eyes, enjoying them as they worked my cock like a pretty little vise.

This was the fucking dream.

With my grip on her hips, I started to work in and out of her, going deep, then pulling out.

My dick was coated in their releases and it turned me on. I couldn't keep up my control and it took only a matter of minutes for me to increase my pace and start to fuck her harder and faster.

The sound of our moans and slapping bodies filled the air. I didn't want this moment to end. I watched her take all of me. Her pussy was designed to take all of us, I just knew it, and tonight, she proved it.

I fucked her harder.

I was so close.

To make it last, I tried to find thoughts that would dampen my arousal, but nothing came to mind. The pleasure, all of Emily, she consumed us all in the best possible way. She'd come back to us, and I knew without a shadow of a doubt that she would forever belong to us.

There was no way this couldn't not work. Staring at my family, and Emily, Gael, River, and Vadik, they were mine as I was theirs. Nothing would ever tear us apart, and I certainly wouldn't let it.

The moment we found our parents, I was going to finally fucking end them. Only two left, and then, the rest of our lives.

Chapter Nineteen

Emily

I couldn't remember a time I'd ever been this happy. As I stared across the room at Caleb, I felt the smile on my lips. This happiness didn't grow on trees and it wasn't inbuilt into anyone. This came about because … I was finally happy here with my four men. It helped having Ashley around, but Gael had told me on more than one occasion that Earl wanted to leave. He was tired of sticking around, and part of me couldn't exactly blame him. Who would want to stay in this shitty town?

I paused in my reading and wondered if I wanted to leave. Growing up, all I envisioned was leaving town, getting out of here, but in truth, that was getting away from the lifestyle of everything we knew.

Tapping my fingers on the book, I glanced over at Caleb. He was writing something down.

"Did you ever think about leaving town?" I asked.

He looked up. "Why would I want to do that?" he asked.

"I don't know. This isn't exactly the best of towns."

He chuckled. "It's our home, Emily. Here, we don't have to hide." He put his pen down. "I have thought about it, though. Getting up. Leaving. Not looking back. I do think about it regularly."

"What stops you?"

"I'm not one of these men who can pretend for shit," he said. "I don't want to rub shoulders with a society I don't trust or believe in. To me, they're the ones living a lie. Here, we're the truth. It's cold, fucking harsh, but it's the truth."

"Wow," I said.

He got up from his seat and moved around the desk, coming straight to the sofa. A petty part of me wanted to scooch on over to stop him, but I restrained myself. I played the good girl role and watched him.

Caleb sighed as he sat down. "We're all killers here, Emily. You know what we have to do. The deals we make. The risks to our lives every single day and we do it willingly. Out there, living a nine-to-five job, pretending I don't know about this, I couldn't do it. I was born and raised to be who I am today." He reached out, stroking a curl back. "I thought you understood?"

"I do. Of course, I do. I don't want you to change. I'd never want that. I just figured you'd want something else."

I waited as he seemed to think about my answer.

"I guess I'm kind of boring. There's nothing in this world I've ever wanted more than to have you." He leaned in close and kissed my lips.

"Well, you've got me. Let's hope you never, ever get bored." I laughed, only partly joking.

"Marry me."

This made me stop, and I stared at him as if he was completely crazy. "What?" There was no way I heard that correctly.

"Marry me, Emily. Make all of us happy men."

"How does me marrying you make them happy men?"

"You want us, we want you. I'm the one who appears in charge. It always looks good on paper."

"Do the others know that you're asking me this right now?"

"Of course."

I turned to see River entering the office. He held a

knife in one hand and a half-eaten apple in the other.

Gael and Vadik were not too far behind him. They were also eating. Vadik handed Caleb a sandwich, while Gael gave one to me.

"Eat up. You're going to need your strength."

I stared down at the sandwich, not knowing if I had the appetite for it. Could I eat it?

Of course, I took a large bite. The largest one of all, chewing on the food, but I didn't swallow. Just kept chewing.

"You can answer me whenever you like."

"I didn't think we were ever going to get married. There are way too many people at this party."

At least Vadik laughed at my reasoning.

"It makes perfect sense to us. You'll wear a ring of all of our choosing, but you'll also be wearing something all of us pick out." River reached into his jacket pocket, got up from the arm of the chair where he was perched, and handed me a long, rectangular box. At first, I looked at it as if it was going to hurt me, which was silly. There was no way anything could hurt me.

Opening the box, I saw a gold bracelet. There was a love heart on the end near the clasp.

"This is what I want you to wear. Caleb said he was going to ask you to marry him today. I wanted to be ready."

"You thought about this?"

"We all did." Gael came to me next, handing me a small square box. Inside lay a pair of pearl earrings. They were so beautiful. Tears filled my eyes.

Vadik was next. This was a thicker-shaped box and when I opened it, a pendant necklace waited for me. "We want you to wear all of these for us," he said. "If you'd take us. Caleb will provide you with the ring, and well, you'll have a part of each of us."

The tears that had filled my eyes spilled over and down my cheeks.

"I thought a marriage proposal was supposed to make women happy?" Gael asked.

I burst out laughing. "I am happy, you idiot. I just … I'm a little speechless. I don't know what to say."

"A yes or no is a good thing," Caleb said. "I'd at least like to add something to your collection."

I looked at my men and I nodded, spilling the word *yes*. I never wanted to lose them and there had been way too many circumstances leading up to me losing them. Nearly dying being the biggest one.

One by one, they each placed their item on me. Caleb came last, sliding the engagement ring onto my finger.

"I … I love you all so much," I said.

"And we love you." They each pulled me into their arms, giving me a kiss, and I fell even deeper in love.

At first, loving all of them had made me a little uncomfortable. It wasn't exactly right, but now, I really didn't give a shit. In fact, I wanted to share the news.

"Can I go and tell Ashley?" she asked.

"Sure." Caleb pulled his cell phone from his pocket and I moved out of the way to dial my best friend.

The happiness I'd felt at the beginning of the day had only grown into a fever pitch. Nothing could take this away from me.

Ashley answered on the third ring and she was more than excited with the news. What was more, she was also thrilled to be helping me plan my wedding.

I was getting married to four amazing guys. I didn't know how I actually got so lucky.

****

Caleb

A couple of days later

"I hear congratulations are in order?" Earl Valentine looked at me across the last abandoned building my father and Gael's father had burned down. While Emily had been high on our proposal, we'd been dealing with the mess my father liked to leave behind.

The man was a fucking menace. He really pissed me off. Ever since Earl had been able to retract the hit on Emily's life, and placed it on my father's, they'd evaded us at every turn.

Only two left, but it seemed they were stealthier than I gave them credit for, which only served to piss me off even more.

Running fingers through my hair, I paced back to my car.

"Don't worry, Ashley has already told us we've got an invitation."

"I'm not interested in making small talk with you."

"No, but you're always interested when I can help you."

I glared at him. "Do you have a natural way of pissing people off?"

"You tell me."

"You promised me you'd help me."

"I have by far exceeded my part in this agreement."

"Then why are you sticking around?"

"I'm not an idiot. If Daniel and Dean actually pull this off and get the drop on your woman, and you four, which I didn't think was possible but now I'm more convinced of it than ever, who do you think they're coming after next?" He tilted his head to the side. "I'm not sticking around for the thrilling company, Caleb. I'm here to clean up a loose end. The fact he can do this in your town simply means you don't have as much control as you think."

I rammed my fist into his face. I didn't need to hear all of my shortcomings, and especially from this prick with a virgin complex.

"You can fuck off out of my town the moment you like. I don't want nor do I need you here, you piece of shit. You're nothing and I don't want you here causing trouble."

My punch had sent him to the ground and he released a chuckle. "You need to learn to keep a hold of your temper." He got to his feet.

I'd had enough. Rather than punch him again, I left him alone and went to my car. We'd driven together. Gael, Vadik, and River were each handling different assignments I'd given them. Just because Emily was back didn't mean our business had ended. We still had money to collect, punishments to dole out, and statements to make.

Our fathers were always busy dealing with their reputation. In no way could the Monsters' Crew fall. That was always the name of the game. I had thought my father overreacted when I was younger, but now, I knew the truth. I knew what the world was capable of, and we were the biggest targets all the time.

Drake was the one who constantly kept our asses safe.

Earl climbed into the passenger seat of the car. "We know they're in town."

"Of course, they're in fucking town," I said. "The moment they leave, they've got plenty of hits on their head, and there's not a fucking thing we can do about it." I was so pissed off. Angry, in fact. They were teasing us, just like we'd played with them. This was a game to them.

They weren't even burning down or destroying buildings of any real value. What they were doing was complete and total horseshit. They needed to be stopped. I didn't know how I was going to do it.

When I arrived home, Earl followed me inside.

The entire house was quiet. Guards were still at the doors and they acknowledged me as I passed. I immediately went to my office and to my drinks table. The only way to come back from this was to have a nice, hard, stiff drink.

"Are there any places you haven't looked?" Earl asked.

"Be quiet."

"Be careful how you speak to me, boy. A little respect goes a long way. Remember, I didn't have to come to you."

"I seem to recall threatening to blow your fucking boat up," I said. "And you were in shark-infested waters. I don't think you would've lasted long."

He laughed. "Do you think that scares me? I know for a fact you wouldn't have done that."

"And why is that?"

The smile on his face made me want to punch him again. There was only a slight reddening from the blow I'd landed on him less than an hour ago. I was starting to think this prick was invincible.

"Ashley. You can hate me all you want, but I knew what she meant to Emily, and there was no way you were going to allow anyone to hurt her. Least of all yourself."

"Do you think I couldn't have covered it up?" I asked.

"You could, but you see, that would have made you a liar. I've seen the way you look at that woman, and it's with stars in your eyes. Always." He laughed. "Be careful, people may start to see you as weak."

"What do you think they see you as?"

"Because of my need to have an innocent woman?" Earl asked. "The difference between me and you is I don't care. I take what I want, the consequences be damned."

"I wonder if you'll feel this way when you fall in love," I said. I didn't care if he loved Ashley or not. I'd already made the necessary arrangements for when he tossed her aside like trash. I knew deep in my heart Emily would never forgive me. It meant Earl was right. I'd never do anything to hurt her, and purposefully killing her best friend wouldn't exactly win me rewards. I had to be smart when it came to Emily. Win her over the only way I knew how, and that was to be honest with her.

"As thrilling as this is, I want to take Ashley back home." Earl got to his feet.

They'd overrun a hotel building. No one was allowed to take a room while he was there.

I was about to say something to piss him off when the door opened. Ashley stood with a smile but soon frowned when she saw me. "When did you return?"

"Just now. Our final building was a bust. They'd burned it down to nothing. It's going to take a lot of money to do some rebuilds." I was only grateful that so far, my father was happy to irritate me, not to kill any more of my men.

Ashley shook her head. "Wait, what?"

"What is it?" Earl asked. He went to Ashley's side and I saw the way she tensed and his jaw clenched.

What the hell did that mean?

Ashley looked from me to Earl. "Emily got a letter with a single white rose. It told her to meet you at the family graveyard." She looked between us. "She's been gone an hour. "Tell me you were there."

My blood ran cold.

"Show me this letter," I said.

Ashley rushed out of the room and I followed closely behind her. She handed me the small rectangular letter. It wasn't my writing, but I recognized it instantly.

"Where's Drake?" I asked, already heading toward the door.

"He got a call before Emily saw this, from you."

"I didn't fucking call him."

They had her and because I'd been too damn focused on finding them myself, I'd put her in fucking danger.

I was an asshole.

Chapter Twenty

Emily

Pain.

That was all I felt.

In my head. All over my face. My back where he'd landed a blow.

They'd also stripped me down to my underwear. So far, they hadn't gone far, but I'd curled up in a ball, hating myself so damn much.

When I got the rose and the letter, it had confused me, but rather than question it or wait for Drake to return, I'd followed the directions.

Big fucking mistake.

The moment I walked into the graveyard, Daniel and Dean had been waiting. They'd slammed me against a tree, I'd been punched in the head, and then dragged to this crypt. I'd never seen the family graveyard before. It was nearly a ten-minute walk from the house, and that was if you were speed-walking.

Crypts and graveyards freaked me out in a big way.

"I wonder what they will think when they find your body," Daniel said. "What I can't decide is if I should cut you up, fuck you, and then slit your throat."

"It has been years since I've fucked someone covered in blood," Dean said.

"You were always a sick and horny fucker." Daniel looked toward his friend with affection.

"Takes one to know one."

Daniel crouched down on the floor next to me and ran a finger down my body, going from my neck, sliding down toward my thigh. He grabbed my thigh, his fingers digging in so deep that I whimpered.

He enjoyed this. Relished my pain. I couldn't stand it, but I put up with it. Not making a sound. Accepting what he was doing to me. I'd been too dazed from the blows to the head.

This wasn't me. I knew this. I was a fighter. I didn't quit, and yet here I lay as if I'd given up. As if I'd given them the key to my soul.

I closed my eyes as he released me.

If they didn't find me soon, I was going to die. I knew that.

The sound of metal on stone forced me to open my eyes. Dean approached. He carried a blade in his grip and he smiled at me.

"You know, River was taken once. He was held in a similar place to this, bound, tortured. All because your fucking dad ordered it! I should do to you what was done to him. Make you pay for your father's sins. I should have killed you when I had the chance." The tip of the blade pressed against the skin of my stomach. I tried not to breathe but panic began to build within me. I was terrified, and as he pressed the blade to my skin, I released a whimper.

"I wonder if seeing you all cut up will remind him of what happened to him." He pushed the blade against my skin, not stabbing me but nicking my skin so it hurt so damn badly.

Tears filled my eyes. "Please," I said.

"Are you going to beg us to stop, is that what is about to happen?" he asked.

I'd begged my father until I'd stopped. He never did. The beatings came regardless and even now, if I begged them, pleaded with them, offered them whatever it was they wanted on a silver platter, I knew they wouldn't care. None of them would. They wanted to see me hurt. To watch my pain.

I couldn't give them the satisfaction.

All I could do was accept the pain.

Endure the suffering.

I stilled as he moved to another part of my body. The blade pierced my skin. I screamed. I didn't know how long I'd be able to take this.

Fight!

I didn't have to lie down.

They were going to kill me regardless. Why not surprise them in the process?

With my screams, I kept them distracted. I used my hand to try to find something to hit them with. I reached out, trying to grab something, anything, and when I felt a rock, I grabbed it and slammed it against Dean's head, knocking him backward. In the process, he dropped the knife. Before Daniel could get it, I had it within my grasp and I got to my feet, glaring at them.

"I bet you weren't expecting that."

I felt the blood from my wounds dripping down my flesh. It made me want to vomit, but somehow, I kept it all inside and glared at both of them.

I waited. Desperate for one or more of them to attack me.

Daniel came in first, but I was no match for him. I was able to swipe him with the blade, but as I went left, he moved right, grabbing me around the waist. His grip was too tight, and Dean came at me, backhanding me as he took the knife from me. Before I knew what was happening, he'd stabbed me in the shoulder.

I yelled.

If anyone was near, they had to have heard it.

He pulled the blade out and Daniel tossed me to the floor, kicking me in the back. I tried to scramble away, but he grabbed me by my hair, pulling my head back. "I don't mind fucking a corpse," he said.

He tilted my head back more and Dean handed him the blade. It came close to my neck and then a gun went off. The blade dropped down to the ground, and me along with it. I shivered as the sudden cold filled the room.

I didn't exactly know what happened next as warmth surrounded me.

After everything I'd just been through, I closed my eyes for only a moment, but when I opened them again, I saw the sky.

Was I dead?

I didn't know.

It was okay to close my eyes.

To go to sleep.

The pain would kill me soon.

****

Gael

I sat in our woman's private hospital room.

She'd lost a great deal of blood.

For at least an hour, my dad and Caleb's dad had been beating her, hurting her. She had bruises, missing clumps of hair, and knife wounds.

Caleb and Earl had gotten to her first. Leaning forward, I put my elbows on my knees and prayed. That was all I did. I didn't know if anyone listened, but I hoped they wouldn't take our woman away.

I couldn't stand it.

Drake was in the other room. We'd tracked him through the GPS on his cell phone to a bar in town. Our dads' final contacts were waiting. They'd beaten him up good. He'd been strung up and used as a piñata.

He had internal bleeding and so far, he hadn't regained consciousness.

There was a time I didn't think I could trust him,

but now, I knew without a doubt, he was loyal to us. We would take care of him.

He'd never be a Monster, but he was family.

"Any change?" Vadik asked, handing me a coffee.

"No."

"Ashley's been given a sedative," River said, coming into the room. "She can't handle this at the moment. She feels responsible because she didn't tell Emily to wait to speak to us." He ran a hand down his face. "How is she?"

"No change," I said. "Is Caleb dealing with the paperwork?"

"Yep," Vadik said. "They always want to make sure they get their money, don't they?"

"Do you think she's going to want to stick around and marry us?" I asked. I didn't want to speak the words out loud, but I didn't know what else to say. I loved my woman more than anything. Had been in love with her all this time. I knew to the outside world, this was fucked up and there was no way it could work, but I said fuck them. They didn't know us. They didn't know what we were capable of. If I said we could make this work, then that was exactly what we were going to do. No one could stop us.

Emily belonged to us.

"I hope so," Vadik said. "She knows how we feel about her. That's never going to change. We all love her."

"And our dads are out of the way. The threat to her life is over."

"The threat in Crude Hill never ceases."

"No, but it doesn't matter where she goes, does it? We're the ones who love her. Everyone else, they couldn't protect her like we do."

I wanted to dispute River. We hadn't exactly done a good job in protecting her today.

"Let's wait until she wakes up and deal with whatever she has to say when it happens," Vadik said.

The voice of reason.

I sipped at my coffee and watched her. She looked so peaceful, but with each hour that passed, more of the bruising came out even worse than before. I couldn't stand to see her in pain. I wanted to take it away.

There was nothing I could think of that would do that.

Seconds passed until Caleb finally arrived. "Everything has been handled." He took the last seat. Two of us were on each side of her bed.

"What happened to the graveyard?" I asked. I had to talk or do something. I couldn't handle this.

"I've arranged to have it torn down," Caleb said. "Their bodies have already been taken care of, burned. The ashes will be left in an urn, along with Ace's and Marshall's."

"We're not keeping their ashes," I said. "Throw them into the dirt where they belong."

"Already plan to. I figured we could have a nice little ceremony." Caleb smiled.

I didn't feel like smiling. Our woman was hurt and for me, that was no matter to laugh at or rejoice. I hated it. We'd caused that.

"She's going to wake up," Caleb said.

"I know she's going to wake up. What I care about is what she's going to want to do when she does wake up. What if she doesn't want us?" I asked. "What if she can't stand to be around us?"

"Not going to happen," Emily said.

At first, I didn't even realize she'd spoken, then,

along with the other three, I got to my feet and moved toward the bed. She was awake.

She offered me a smile but then winced. "My face."

"Don't worry about it." I took her hand within mine, kneeling beside her bed. She turned her head toward me.

"Please don't worry, Gael."

"I can't lose you."

"You're not going to."

I didn't want to put my fears into words in case they gave her an idea. That was the last thing I wanted to do. If she hadn't thought about leaving, then I certainly didn't want to give her the idea.

"I love you."

"I love you too." She gave my hand a squeeze. "Are they gone?"

"Yes," Caleb said. "All you have to do is rest."

"I can't rest while you're all worrying over me. I'm fine."

"We know," we all said in unison.

"No, I mean I'm not going to leave." She turned her head back to me. "I heard you, and I'm not going to go anywhere. You think I don't know the risks involved with belonging to you guys? You're going to upset a lot of people, and I may be a target, but as I've told you so many times, I can't walk away from you. What's more, I don't want to. This is a weird setup, but it's our setup and I love it."

I couldn't help it, I got to my feet and I leaned down, kissing her lips. "Did I tell you I love you?"

"Not enough. You need to tell me every single hour of every day," she said.

I laughed. "You can count on it. I promise you, you'll never go a single day without knowing how I feel."

"How we all feel," Vadik said.

I agreed with them.

"I hate hospitals," she said.

"Soon, you can leave," Caleb said.

She nodded and sighed. "I'm starving. Do you know where Ashley is?"

I held her hand as Caleb filled in the blanks. He told her about Ashley's upset and Drake's beating. Like a true Monsters' Queen, she handled it. From this day forward, I promised myself I was never going to underestimate her. She could handle whatever we threw at her.

Chapter Twenty-One

Emily

I'd been given the all-clear to go home, along with some interesting news, which I got to share with my guys. Vadik was cleaning my room and Gael waited outside while Caleb and River had gotten the car. They weren't trusting anyone with my safety, and I stood in Drake's room, which was why Gael was outside.

My men had seen fit to keep me in the hospital for a week. I didn't need it, but they felt they had no choice but to keep me in for as long as possible. In that time, Drake had woken from his coma. The moment he did, he'd freaked out. My room had been right next to his, and the nurses had no choice but to sedate him.

"I know you're in my room," Drake said.

His eyes were closed.

I thought I'd taken a beating, but nothing to this extent.

He had two broken legs, a broken arm, cracked ribs; I thought I heard a ruptured spleen, internal bleeding, and two bruised eyes. I saw when he opened at least one. I understood the pain in them.

"Hey," I said.

"Hey. I bet you thought I was still a traitor, huh?" he asked.

I shook my head. "No, I didn't." I moved toward the bed. "May I?" I asked, pointing at the chair. I'd been tempted to sit on the bed, but I knew if I moved it, I'd only cause him pain, and I couldn't do that to him.

"Be my guest, I wouldn't stop you."

"If you don't want me here, tell me to leave."

"Emily, you hated me, not the other way around. I don't have a crush on you, nor do I want to get into your pants, but you know that."

I laughed. "They showed me what was happening to you. I'm so sorry I couldn't help."

"It's fine. I've always been told I need a beatdown. Just didn't expect to explode with candy." He winced.

"You don't have to move." I put my hand on top of his. "I'm so sorry."

"Emily, your men gave me the job to protect you. I know to many it would be seen as a babysitting job, but over the years, I knew how important you were. I wasn't given a job that I saw as less. I was given the ultimate job. I take your protection seriously and the fact I..." He stopped and his jaw clenched.

"Drake, you didn't cause this. None of this was your fault."

"But I shouldn't have answered that fucking call."

I started to cry. My emotions were going to get crazy for the next nine months. "Hindsight is a beautiful thing, isn't it? It makes us question ourselves all the time, but we can't stop what happened. There's no way to change it. We can only learn from our mistakes." I stroked my thumb back and forth across his knuckles. "Thank you so much for being loyal to my men. For giving them a chance, for being there for them. They don't have anyone like you, and for that, you have all of my trust. I have faith in you, Drake. Thank you so much."

"I don't cry."

"Don't worry. I'll cry for the both of us," she said.

He looked at me. "Does that mean what I think it means?"

"I'm pregnant. The doctors took a blood test. I'm

going to be a mom and my men are going to be dads."

"I'll feel sorry if it's a girl," he said.

I burst out laughing and he groaned.

"Enough," she said. "We have to stop talking now. Enough is enough."

For the next ten minutes, I sat with him, listening to the machines beep around him. A nurse came in to check on him, and Drake's pain took him to sleep.

I stayed with him, not wanting him to leave him alone.

Time passed until Gael, Vadik, Caleb, and River entered the room. None of us spoke. Drake was still fast asleep.

"You know, I thought you were crazy hiring him," I said.

"We all did," River said.

I glanced toward my men. They were all staring right back at me. "He's loyal to you guys. We've got to take care of him. Make sure he's safe and protected. We can't let anything else happen to him." I needed to make it up to him so he knew I trusted him. I didn't know if Drake even cared about my thoughts, but I felt the need to make it right.

"Drake will always have a job, Emily. Always," Caleb said.

"Good." I laughed. "I don't think I'll be fixing him up with a girl anytime soon." I was so not a matchmaker. My body had started to heal, but still, all I wanted to do was get out of here. I hated hospitals. "Can we go?" I asked.

Gael came to me, helping me up.

"It's time for us to go home," Caleb said.

I stilled, looking at the door then at my men. Home. It was such an innocent word, and yet, it was entirely what I needed to hear.

****

Vadik

One week later

We found the perfect spot for the ashes.

All six of us, me, Gael, River, Caleb, Emily, and Ashley, we carried the urn into the deepest part of the words on the edge of Crude Hill. We were dressed in sweats and shirts. It was cold and dirty.

I held on to Emily as she kept on slipping over.

When we'd gotten home from the hospital, she didn't waste any time in telling us the good news. She carried our baby.

I'd never been so freaking happy or scared at the same time than at that moment. This overwhelming need to protect her had struck me. It had been even harder than any other time.

All I knew was … we'd do whatever it took to make her safe. Caleb was having the hardest time. I'd found him in the library on many occasions, looking at the picture of his mother. We'd all wanted Emily pregnant, but now there was a real threat. Women didn't make it in childbirth, even now. All we could do was be there and fucking hope she made it through.

"Are you okay?" I asked.

The ground was way too wet and too easy to slip over. "Yeah, I'm fine. It's kind of morbid, though, right? We're walking out to give your fathers a fitting sendoff?"

"They're rotting in hell. We're just putting them where they belong," Gael said.

I couldn't agree more.

We came to a spot where there was at least a couple of feet between trees. It looked like the wildlife used it to take shits, which was all the more fitting.

River was the one who carried the shovel, and at

Caleb's nod, he dug into the ground. He only dug a couple of shovels in. There was no need to do back-breaking labor for this sendoff.

"You don't think this is going to make us cursed, do you?" Ashley asked. When we got back, Earl wasn't going to be sticking around. He and intended to take Ashley back to wherever he lived.

I didn't like it. I knew Emily even more so. We all didn't like Earl, but he'd been with Caleb and had been the one to carry Emily to safety, so we couldn't complain too much.

He'd helped us when he could have turned his back and for that, we had to at least give him a chance.

"Please, you believe in that shit?" Gael asked.

"I don't know. Coming here was supposed to be good luck. I don't think any of what has happened so far has been luck."

"We met each other," Emily said, moving toward her best friend.

Ashley chuckled. "You couldn't stand me."

"That's not completely true. I was trying to survive and you were like bait in a tank full of sharks."

They both hugged and laughed. "I guess. Sure. I can see that. Fine."

"If we're cursed, doing this wouldn't give me so much happiness," Caleb said, tipping the contents of the urn into the dirt. Rather than using the shovel to put the mud back, he kicked it with his boot and started to stomp all over the mess.

We all joined in, grinding the mud into the ashes that were once our fathers. It wasn't exactly the most respectful sendoff, but it was the best they were going to get.

I had no regrets.

Once the ashes and mud had mingled together,

we all headed out to where Earl was already waiting with the car. He didn't hold his hand out to Ashley, just looked at her.

"This is my stop." She hugged Emily tight to her. "Take care and send me pictures every single day."

"If he hurts you, you come to us. Promise me."

"I promise." Ashley kissed her friend's cheek and I held on to Emily as Ashley climbed into the car.

Earl came toward us, shaking each of our hands in turn.

"Gentlemen," he said before getting into the car as well.

It was anticlimactic, but after everything we'd been through already, I didn't need any additional drama.

Emily held her hand up and we all waved goodbye.

She didn't move until their cars could no longer be seen. Finally, she turned toward us. "What happens now?"

Caleb came forward, pulling her in close. "Now, we go home, plan our wedding, then prepare for our baby."

"Really?" she asked.

"Also, we've got to pick up Drake. He's coming home and he's requesting we bring the nurse who has been helping him get better," Gael said.

Emily chuckled. "I can't believe it's all over."

"It's not over," River said. "Crude Hill High is back open. Shit still needs to be done, and the Monsters, well, we're the kings of the castle."

Emily pressed the back of her palm to my chest, rolling her eyes. "Come on, it's time to go home."

And that was something I was looking forward to.

Epilogue One

River

Eight months later

Emily's scream echoed around the room. The midwife and doctor were there. Her water had broken and the contractions had gone from being minutes apart to only seconds. She'd been in pain so Caleb had gone to get them both, but now, she was having a very natural birth, with nothing to help ease the pain, and I hated myself.

Glancing at Gael, Vadik, and Caleb, I saw we were all in a great deal of pain for her.

"You've got to push, Emily," the midwife said.

"I am pushing. Ouch. It hurts. No. No. No. He can just stay up there. It's safe for him there."

I moved to her side and even as she squeezed my hand in a death grip, I didn't care.

"I love you, baby, I love you so much."

All four of us moved close, trying to be the ones to take her pain away, but it wasn't happening.

"You all did this." She sobbed.

"Push, baby," Caleb said.

"Fuck off!"

I would've smiled if I didn't fear for her. She'd spent the last couple of months ordering us not to curse in front of our child. Now, she was the one cursing.

"Push, Emily," the doctor said.

I expected her to rant at him.

Instead, she took a deep breath and moved. Her hand clasped mine, and she was fucking strong.

I encouraged her, we all did, and she pushed. Her face turned an odd shade of red before she collapsed to the bed, and then came the beautiful sound of a baby screaming. I kept my gaze on Emily. With four of us, I knew one of us would check on the baby.

Her face was covered in perspiration.

"Is he okay?" Her voice was hoarse from the screaming.

The sounds of his screams filled the air, and I knew she'd started to panic, which wasn't good.

"They've got him."

"But…" She sniffed.

"You have got a beautiful baby boy, Emily."

"I do?" A cute bundle wrapped in a white towel was placed in her arms.

"Oh my," she said. "He's so beautiful."

I was scared to say anything, and Emily tilted her head back, smiling at us all. "Do you see him?"

We crowded around her, taking in the sight of our son. His face was scrunched up, but he was so perfect.

"I love him so much."

"You did good," I said.

She laughed. "I was horrible."

We all denied it, and she shook her head. "Next time, I need to be in the hospital."

"You did well, Emily," the midwife said.

"Thank you."

There was a knock at the door. The doctor answered and Drake came in. It had been a tough year for our friend. He'd had to do endless hours of physical therapy and he still had to walk around with a cane. I knew it made him angry. He was taking a lot more time to heal than he'd like.

"You're okay?" Drake asked.

In the past eight months, Emily hadn't been offended or pushed aside because of Drake's moods. She'd been determined to bring him out of his shell, which was exactly what she'd done.

"Come and see."

She'd been covered. I didn't go far, but Drake had enough room to see.

"He looks … like a baby," Drake said.

"Stop it, he's perfect."

"The next generation."

"Yeah, it won't be long before he'll be walking the walls of Crude Hill High, being just as stubborn as his dads." She leaned down, rubbing her nose against her son before looking up. "I'm so looking forward to making more."

Drake stepped back as we all surrounded our woman.

I didn't know what we'd done to deserve her. We were Monsters, through and through. She had no real idea of the damage we did to keep her safe. Our reputations were worse than our fathers, but she was our gift, and I would cherish her always.

Epilogue Two

Ashley

Nine months before

I didn't like how I'd left things with Emily.

It wasn't her fault that her dad was a complete and total ass who couldn't keep it in his pants. My mom had been looking for love, and she had gotten it, as well as an easy life, but it had cost her big time: it had cost her her life. My friendship with Emily had saved me. Sometimes I couldn't handle the guilt. It got to be a little too much for me.

The last seven years had sucked, big time. I knew that. I'd listened to her cry because she'd lost not one, but four men. Sure, they were Monsters and were used to doing evil things, but what I'd gotten used to was that Emily came from that world. I didn't.

My life was more about worrying when the next meal was going to arrive, or if my mom could hold down a job for longer than a couple of months. It had all changed with Emily's dad.

Pushing those thoughts to one side, I tried not to worry about the client who wanted to talk about my first course. I'd been offered the chance to do the first courses at the restaurant, which was a big deal for me. Now someone had a complaint. That was why they called out the chefs, right?

I felt sick to my stomach.

I didn't want to lose this job. It wasn't my dream, but it was the next best thing. Cooking food was my life. It was what brought me so much joy and how I tried to make Emily happy.

The client had decided to sit in the VIP section of the restaurant. It was rather dark, and I noticed not many people were around.

Approaching the table number I'd been given, I saw a man in the shadows.

"Hi, I'm Ash— I mean, Harper Coast. You wanted to see me?"

All of a sudden, something covered my mouth. I couldn't shout or scream. Everything was muffled and going dark quickly. The man in the corner came into sight and I knew who he was.

Earl Valentine.

What the fuck did he want with me?

Everything went black.

Author Note:

Crude Hill High will return with Ashley's book. I'm so excited to share her and Earl's story with you. It will be an older man tale, which I love. After their story, I will be heading back to school, where lots of people are calling for their stories to be told.

www.samcrescent.com

EVERNIGHT PUBLISHING ®

www.evernightpublishing.com

Printed in Great Britain
by Amazon